NAKED MAGAZINE'S REAL STORIES

ENCOUNTERS AND ADVENTURES

NAKED MAGAZINE'S REAL STORIES

ENCOUNTERS AND ADVENTURES

A Collection of True Stories

From Our Naked Magazine Readers

FIRST EDITION
VOLUMES 1.1-2.1

A Boner Book by
The Nazca Plains Corporation
Las Vegas, Nevada
2004

ISBN:1-887895-40-X

Published by,

The Nazca Plains Corporation ®
4640 Paradise Rd, Suite 141
Las Vegas NV 89109-8000

PUBLISHER'S NOTE
This is a work of fiction. Names, characters, places, and incidents either are the products of the writer's imagination or are used fictitiously, and any resemblance to actual persons, living or dead, business establishments, events or locales is entirely coincidental.

Editor, Kyler O'Leary

Photographer, Robert Bishop

Cover Model, Jayden

Cover Designer, Kyler O'Leary

For Our Naked Reader's

Introduction

Since the very first issue, the readers of Naked Magazine have sent in their Encounters and Adventures for publicatoin in the magazine. We found some of these stories much too "hot" to publish, but we kept them in the back of the filing cabinet - - until now! We brought them out, dusted them off and here they are totally uncut in their original versions.

If they turn you on, titillate your own fantasies or even get you to take pen in hand and write down your own experiences, then we have accomplished our mission. We want to hear about your Encounters and Adventures so get them to us:

The Editor
Naked Magazine
4640 Paradise Rd, Suite 141
Las Vegas, NV 89109-8000

Who knows? You might just find it published in Naked Magazine!

We hope you will enjoy these stories again if you first read them with Naked Magazine, and if you are a first time reader, then sit back and enjoy the most hilarious, craziest, and erotic true nudist stories ever!

Robert Steele, Publisher

Contents

ATTENTION
BEYOND THIS POINT
YOU MAY ENCOUNTER
NUDE SUNBATHERS

NAKED MAGAZINE'S REAL STORIES

ENCOUNTERS AND ADVENTURES

FIRST EDITION
VOLUMES 1.1 - 2.1

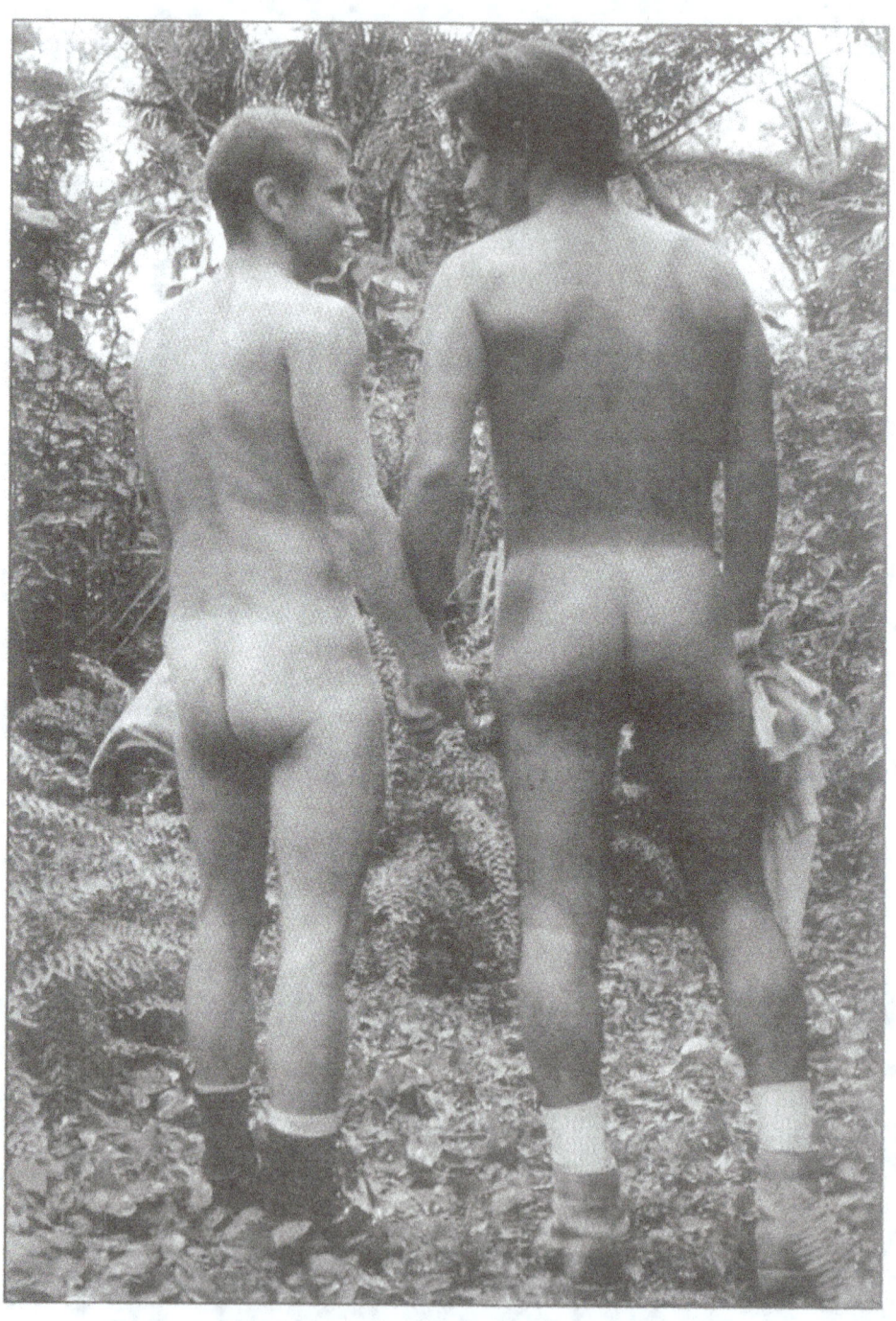

MOUNTAIN LOVERS

DEAR **NAKED MAGAZINE,**

Here is a story I would like to share with your readers. My lover John and I are both nudists. We're naked at home most of the time. We enjoy driving naked, going to nude beaches and attending naked parties. It's not so much a sexual thing, but rather a way of life.

One day recently though, we had one of the most exciting and romantic naked days of our relationship. It was a beautiful Saturday morning. A few days earlier a large storm had dumped several inches of rain and a couple feet of snow in the mountains. By Saturday however, a warm front had come in pushing the mid-day temperature into the low 70s. That morning the sky was so blue and the air was crisp and clean. We decided it was a good day to go hiking in the mountains.

I packed a light lunch for both of us and threw an old blanket and a couple of towels into a backpack. John started to put on a pair of shorts. "No way", I said. "It's too nice out for clothes. We're going naked today!" We put our shorts in the backpack just in case of emergency and headed out the back door. We had driven home naked from the mountains and the beach several times before but this had an overwhelming sense of excitement and danger for us both.

We got in our pickup and I, as usual, popped an instant hard on. It always happens at first and then I relax a bit and it goes away. By the time we were out of the garage and half way down the block, I was back to my soft self. John is very nervous anytime we drive naked. He is always worried that someone will see inside the cab of our truck. Each time I reassure him and remind him that we are up high enough and the windows are tinted. No one will see in.

A mile or so from home he was relaxing and enjoying the riskiness of it all. We drove through town over Laurel Canyon towards the 134 freeway. A Natalie Cole cassette played softly on the radio. A feeling of romance started mixing with the air of excitement. Traffic was especially heavy on the freeway and we were stopped bumper to bumper more than a couple of times. It didn't matter though, we sat holding hands and listening to the music.

We headed up the 2 north and entered Angeles National Forest. The traffic we left behind gave way to empty winding roads. It seemed we were the only two people in the park. Posted signs warned us that icy roads may lie ahead. It was true. The roads had been cleared for the most part but there were some slippery spots. I was imagining the truck careening off the road, getting stuck in a snow drift and us naked, screaming for help. The day was too beautiful and we were too horny to worry about getting stuck.

We rounded a huge curve and were faced with a most magnificent sight. The mountains were covered with snow. The white snow against the blue sky was positively inspirational. We pulled off the road towards our favorite spot and parked. We got out of the truck dressed only in our hiking boots. We grabbed the backpack and cooler and started on our hike.

The mixture of the warm sun and cool air felt wonderful against our naked skin. We hiked up a large hill. About a half mile into the hike we found a clear area away from the melting snow and laid out our blanket. Knowing we were the only people within several miles, we set down the rest of our gear and continued hiking naked, leaving what little clothing we had behind. The thrill of being exposed to nature and other possible hikers was more than we could stand.

We made passionate love several times that day on the hills and in the woods surrounding our tiny camp site. As the day grew later, John and I ate our lunch and packed up our belongings. We headed back home still naked. We stayed that way for the rest of the weekend. We renewed a love and a common bond that we have shared throughout our six year relationship. I don't know if we will be able to recreate that special day, but we're gonna try!

- Naked Couple from LA.

REAR OF THE THEATER

DEAR **NAKED MAGAZINE**,

A few years ago-actually more like a decade ago-there was a theatre in Los Angeles called the Oriental, on Sunset Blvd. It was a second run house, the kind that show movies at discount prices, so you could see two movies for just $1.50. During the sweltering months of summer, when the dry heat and blinding glare of the day became almost intolerable, the air-conditioned darkness of the auditorium was a refuge.

Another thing that added to its appeal was that it was often kind of cruisy and despite coolness of the theatre, things in the back row could get quite hot. Although it was on the west side of town, the legions of gays who make their home there, had either not discovered it (which was unlikely) or had written it off because the clientele was generally older. I remember going there one particular warm afternoon. I even remember the movie; it was Barry Levinson's Diner.

There weren't many people in the theatre, but as my eyes adjusted to the darkness, I was able to make out a lone figure in the back row. I took my place a few seats away from him, but determined by the light from the screen that for now, I would be better entertained by the movie, boy was I mistaken. To my astonishment, he was removing his clothes. I watched as he casually took off his pants, folded them neatly and placed them on the seat beside him. Next, he removed his shirt. Then in one quick motion, he slipped off his underwear. He laid back in his seat, stretched out and relaxed as if though he were at home. I took in this whole scene with amazement and disbelief.

I looked around to see if anyone else had witnessed it, but no one had. We were virtually alone at the rear of the theatre. It was clear, however, that the man knew I had seen him strip, and that was exactly what he'd intended. I was fascinated by his nakedness, and couldn't take my eyes off him.

I found myself becoming aroused, not so much by the man himself, who was actually older and not particularly attractive, but by his audacity, and by the fact that he was totally naked in a very public place. Although I had been in that theatre many times, it had never occurred to me to get naked there.

Encouraged by his action, I decided to do the same. I had dressed appropriately for the weather, so my loose-fitting t-shirt came off with little effort, and the thin cotton shorts I wore slipped off with just a tug. Anticipating that I might have an encounter that day, I hadn't worn any underwear. I decided to keep on my well-weathered Birkenstocks against the stickiness of the floor. Throughout this, the man watched me and slowly stroked his dick.

The absence of anyone nearby and the dimness of the light from the screen encouraged me even further. I stood up and walked casually towards the man. He sat up in his seat and looked me over. I pretended to be uninterested in him or his nakedness, and begged his pardon as I passed in front of him-my naked butt just inches from his face. I went out into the aisle and thought about walking to the doors.

My heart was pounding like mad, both from excitement of being naked, and the fear that at any moment the doors might open and I would be caught like a deer in headlights. That prospect forced me back toward my seat. This time as I approached the man, he stood up courteously, and as I passed in front of him, he pressed himself against me. I felt his dick against my butt and his warm breath on the back of my neck. I turned around to face him and our stiff cocks collided. I grabbed his dick and stroked it.

I was just about to go down on him when suddenly the scene in the movie changed from night to brightness of morning! It was as though someone had turned the house lights on! My heart leaped, and my dick fell, and I dove into the seat beside him. It was only then that I realized there was someone seated just two rows directly ahead of us! My mind was racing. Had that person taken all this in? I looked around frantically to see if perhaps there were others who had observed me, but whose presence I had overlooked.

I reached for my shorts. When I turned to look at the man, he was smiling broadly, almost laughing, amused at my panic. He had remained calm and his broad smile put me at ease and provoked a smile in me. He stopped me from putting on my shorts. "It's okay," he whispered reassuringly, "nobody saw you." I composed myself and sat up in the seat.

We sat for a few minutes watching the movie; both of us still naked. Soon he began caressing my chest, tweaking my nipples, then he moved to my belly, then my cock. I soon regained my hard-on. He had never lost his. He wasn't in bad shape for a man who, I guessed, might be in his early fifties. He was a bit thick around the middle but not flabby. He had a nice cock, not very long, but thick and uncut. I felt fine stubble at the base where he had shaved his pubic hair. His balls were also hairless and large and they filled my cupped hand like a water balloon filled to the point of bursting. When finally the light from the screen again dimmed, he told me to stand up.

I gestured toward the person seated just a couple of rows ahead. "Don't worry," he whispered, "she's asleep." I peered through the darkness and made out the form of an old woman, slumped in her seat, oblivious to everything. I stood up, more cautiously than before, and began to look around when he put his hands on my hips and abruptly pulled me to him. He devoured my dick in one quick gulp, sucking like a madman. His mouth encased me like a second foreskin.

The guy was a cock-sucker to the first order. His mouth was so tight around me, had I not seen his toothy smile earlier, I would have sworn he hadn't any teeth at all. As he sucked, I could see him furiously beating his own meat. I bent forward and tried to reach for his cock but he brushed my arm away almost angrily.

Under such extraordinary circumstances, I had no staying power. Our nakedness, the proximity to hostile eyes, the utter brazenness of it all, and his superb technique, all contributed to a quick and shuttering release. I held on to his shoulder to keep my balance, and unloaded deep into his throat for what seemed like a very long time. The guy drained me. Soon I felt the warm, wet contents of those ample balls of his pelting my shins and dripping to my feet.

The old guy came with the force and capacity of a horny teenager; my leg was drenched. I felt bad because I'd cum so quickly and didn't get to suck him in return, but the look on his face was hardly one of disappointment. He sat back in his seat and delicately wiped the corner of his mouth with a handkerchief which he produced from nowhere.

I sat next to him for some time and he played with my limp dick. I knew it would be a while before I could get a hard again, much less produce another load. The smell of cum was in the air and the stuff in my sandal was turning sticky. I felt the need to wash. As I began to dress, I expected him to do the same, but he stayed naked and continued to watch the movie.

It was still early and apparently I was to be the first of many encounters for him during the course of the day. I finally stood up, deftly slipping on my shorts as I rose. I put on my shirt inside out as I later discovered and as I left him, I gave his spent cock a gentle and affectionate squeeze.

In the decade since it occurred, this experience remains vivid in my mind, and frequently fuels my autoerotic fantasies. Although I often went back to the Oriental, and had many encounters there before it closed a few years later, I never again met the naked man, nor did I ever have the nerve to repeat my performance of that hot summer afternoon.

- Naked in the Burbs

SEX SHOP

DEAR **NAKED MAGAZINE**,

I love being naked whenever possible. I'd go everywhere naked if I could, but unfortunately there are too many people who would not let me get away with it. But I would like to tell you about one of my naked adventures. One Saturday afternoon I was driving naked on Santa Monica Blvd. in West Hollywood. As I passed an adult novelty shop I noticed a man standing in the parking lot looking over the wall into the street.

I slowed down as I went by and he saw that I was naked. I went around the block and drove by again. I noticed an empty parking space right in front of where he was standing, so I parked. He could see straight into my car. He walked around the wall and up to my car and squatted down on the curb. We talked for a few minutes as I sat there jacking off. He told me his name was Roy and that he worked in the store. He said he had to go back to work but that I should come into the store and see him sometime.

As he went inside, I drove on. The following Monday evening, I decided to go see him. I walked into the store wearing a long t-shirt with no pants or underwear. Roy was working behind the counter in the back of the store. He had a customer with him at the time, so I looked around until the customer left. There was no one else in the back of the store, and all of the display counters were on an angle, making it difficult for anyone in the front of the store to get a good view of anything in between the counters.

I faced Roy and raised the front of my shirt to expose my dick and started stroking it. Roy watched for a couple of minutes until someone came to the rear of the store. I put my shirt back down and pretended to be looking at some merchandise until the customer left. When I turned to face Roy, he was not there. A few seconds later he came from the back room and stood behind the counter again. This time, he lifted his apron to show his dick and balls out of his pants and now he was stroking.

I don't remember who made the first move but we both made our way to the opposite end of the counter. We were standing in the dildo section and played with each other's dicks. I dropped to my knees and started sucking Roy right there in the store. After a couple of minutes, Roy walked behind me, lifted my shirt to my chest, reached around and started jacking me off.

There were other customers and employees no more than 20 feet away but they didn't look in our direction. After a few minutes, I told Roy to stop or I would cum all over the merchandise.

Before I left, I made a date to meet him in the parking lot at 9 PM when he went to lunch. At 9, I was sitting in my car in the parking lot naked. Roy came out and got into the car. I immediately started to drive away. Before we even got out of the lot, Roy began to undress, throwing his clothes in the back seat.

I drove to an area where there were no homes, just businesses next to Warner-Hollywood Studios. As soon as I stopped the car, Roy got out. I shut the engine off, got out and walked around the car to the sidewalk where Roy was standing naked. We were there for fifteen or twenty minutes jacking ourselves off and sucking each others dicks. During this time, three different cars drove by. As each one came by we squatted down next to the car and immediately got back up. Just after we both came, Roy turned around and noticed a homeless person lying on the doorstep behind us. Apparently we didn't wake him up, or he just didn't care what we were doing. We got back in the car and I took Roy back to work. Since then we have become very good friends, but I still go into the store wearing just that t-shirt sometimes.

- Danny from Los Angeles

COLLEGE STUDY TIME

DEAR **NM**,

I'm a college student. I like to look through your latest issue when I'm on my study break. I've kept the magazine hidden from my roommate because I wasn't sure how he'd react. We're pretty close friends, but I still wasn't sure. One night a while back, we were both studying in our room. It was one of those unusually warm nights for the winter but here in Florida it stays pretty nice most of the time. To make things worse, our room doesn't have any air conditioning. We were both trying to write papers for a Geology class and were close to burn out.

I suggested we take a break. Since it was so damn hot in the dorm, we decided to go outside for a bit. We started walking towards the football stadium. It was set back from the main campus and the lack of lights or people made it seem cooler. We were both only wearing shorts, no shoes or shirts. The stadium is outdoors, so we climbed through the bleachers, walked onto the field and sat down on the grass.

The grass was cool and it felt great. We both lay back to look at the stars and lying on the grass was even better. I don't know what got into me (probably remembering your magazine and my situation at hand). I had this incredible urge to take off my shorts. I made a joke to my roommate about it being so secluded here you could run around the field naked. He laughed. We were quiet for a few seconds then he suddenly said "What the fuck, man it's too hot for clothes." He pulled off his shorts. I couldn't believe it!

I immediately did the same. There we were, completely naked, lying in the middle of the football field, looking at the stars. It was incredible. The coolness of the slightly damp grass and the feel of the breeze over my entire body was something I don't remember ever experiencing before. We stayed there for a good half hour. Finally we returned to the dorm, in shorts (damn it!), but ever since then, when it's warm enough, we hang out naked, and a few times we've gone back to the to the football field naked.

PS: My roommate loves your magazine as much as I do.

-Bill from South Florida

EARTHQUAKE!

DEAR **NM**,

I've been a fan of nudism for a while, always nude around my house, going to nude beaches, etc. But the strangest place I was ever nude came about quite by accident (or should I say - an act of God). As everybody knows there was a major earthquake in Los Angeles in January. When it struck, I was, of course, nude in bed. After it stopped, I panicked. I have never felt a quake like that before. I rushed out of bed and headed for the living room. My security system was blaring, as it does when the power goes off, and the sound was making me even more panicked.

It was very dark but I stumbled my way over misplaced furniture and tumbled bookcases and got to the alarm pad. I couldn't see anything, and my hands were shaking too much to punch in the right code to stop the siren. I remembered I had a flashlight just outside my door as I had taken it outside to look for my cat. I was near the door, so I made my way outside, still naked.

The flashlight was on the edge of the porch. Just then there was an after shock and I suppose that is what made my door close. I was locked out. Normally, I would have climbed in through the window, but I was too shaken to try. Besides, there was broken glass all around outside and I didn't want to take any chances.

I didn't know what to do. The neighbors were already coming out and calling to one another to see if everybody was all right. It would only be a matter of minutes before they would come to check on me. As most of my neighbors were elderly women, I didn't know what I was going to do. Just then, I saw the lights of a police car coming down the street asking if everyone was O.K.

I ran to my hedge and crunched down as far as I could. When the car came by, I waved my hands in the air and asked for help. The car stopped and two officers jumped out. I explained to them what happened. One of them gave me his jacket which I wrapped around my waist. They let me sit in the back of the patrol car while they "broke into" my house.

So there I was, naked, in the back of a police car and I wasn't in trouble for it. It was great! Everything's all right now after replacing a few windows, but I did get a small cut on my foot because I didn't have any shoes on throughout this whole ordeal. Anyway, I love telling this story now.

-Naked Guy in LA

LUNCH WITH A VIEW

DEAR **NAKED**,

June 5, 1990, Lunch today was at a local Bar-B-Q house. Three other guys from the office were with me. A group of laborers sat in the booth across the aisle from us, so I made sure my seat gave me the view I wanted. Diagonal from me, and only five feet away, sat a carpenter who was a sight to behold! In his twenties, with dirty-blonde hair, he had the typical build of his trade.

He was dark from his sun exposure. I only wish he hadn't put on a t-shirt to come in here, but that's required. At least it was quite used and very torn. My gaze worked it's way down his torso. Straining against the dirty white cotton shirt and reached his waist. His jeans appeared to have suffered through years of heavy work, or had been at the mercy of his pocket knife many times. They were in shreds. I immediately went to his crotch. His legs were spread and gave me a sight I wasn't ready to see - his balls were in perfect view!

The few threads that remained in this area did nothing to hide his balls that pressed against those threads to escape. Nearly all the sac was visible as they lay against his left leg. Just above, but more protected by the fabric was the outline of his cock. I nearly choked on my sandwich and couldn't break my stare. The others at the table with me were talking about work and, thank God, ignored me.

I'm sure the carpenter noticed my gaze since he soon groped

himself as he extended the right leg into the aisle, shifting the load of his balls and cock so that the head of his prick was now visible! He was uncut. He would casually drop his hand to cover himself if a waitress or customer walked by, but just as quickly uncovered himself as they passed.

His group sat there, having their cigarettes and after lunch talking for what seemed far too short a time. The others in his group either really didn't notice that he was showing, or were very familiar with the sight and paid no attention at all. He got up slowly as they readied to leave, allowing the guy sitting beside him in the booth to leave first, then the others across the table.

He walked away last, and as he did, the view from the rear was as great as from the front. There was almost no fabric on the backside of his jeans, from between the legs to within two inches from his belt line. The threads hung loosely, giving a perfect view of almost all the crack of his ass and lovely slightly hairy cheeks. He glanced back in my direction only once, but smiled his approval that my stare was still on his nearly totally exposed ass.

To say the least, the memory haunted me all afternoon until I finally went to the men's room to take care of the problem.

- Naked Carl

MOTORCYCLE SALUTE

Dear **NAKED MAGAZINE**,

July 25th, 1990 - Driving in to work this morning, about 7:20, on I-85. I noticed a motorcyclist in my rear view mirror. He was too far back to see well, but he was either in shorts, or wearing khaki pants...his legs looked bare. As we moved on, he got closer, and moved to the lane to my right. I nearly lost it as he passed me. He was wearing only shorts and sandals. The shorts were so large he had pulled the legs completely up around his waist and tucked them in to his waistband. His cock and balls were completely exposed and, fortunately for me, hanging to the left side.

He was probably in his twenties, but who can tell through the helmets, which are the law. His brown hair was long enough to stream out the back of the helmet and blow in the breeze like a long scarf. I jockeyed for the best position to maintain the view. He was along beside me and could easily see how interested I was in looking at him. He maintained position for a few seconds, swinging his left knee out as far as possible. I smiled at him and he gave me a quick wave with his right hand. He slowed and as I moved ahead of him, I thought he would be exiting the highway. Instead, he moved behind me, then up on the left side of my car.

He waited for another car to move on in that lane, and then sped up to get up to my window. He steered his bike with his left hand and used his right to reposition his cock and balls to the right where I could nearly reach out and touch them. He stroked himself a couple of times as he stayed with me, then gave me a kind of salute with that right hand and sped off up the highway.

Needless to say, it was a very nice drive in to work that day, and I continued to think about this biker, wondering how many other drivers would be presented such a nice show as he headed on his northbound journey.

- Naked Carl

ACCIDENTAL PUBLIC INDECENCY

Dear **Naked**,

May 18, 1991 - Tonight, I'd come out to visit a few bars. I really shouldn't have since there was rain in the area, but I'd done it anyway. The night had been frustrating since there was no action whatsoever. By midnight, I was ready to go home, but still wanting some excitement, so I decided to drive home naked.

As is my habit in town, I pulled into a mall and parked near the all night drugstore. I stripped off with the truck door open and was just rolling up my pants when a car pulled by me from the driveway behind the building. I'd completely forgotten about that as an exit from the bar back there. It was a surprise, but apparently they didn't notice what I was doing since they drove on.

It was fun, as usual, driving down 1-85 stark naked! I love the moments when you pass under lighting that makes it possible for someone to potentially see into the truck. I try to be beside big rigs or vans when this happens. By this time of night, there wasn't much traffic. I was in the last mile of the trip to the house when I saw the blue lights. There were two cop cars, one on each side of the road, ahead of me. It was a routine check, not unusual on a Saturday night, they were looking for drunks.

But, here I was, stark naked, no roads off either side of where I could dodge to get dressed. I could only go on. As I braked to a stop at the cop, I put the bag containing my clothes in my lap. The cop asked me for my drivers license and insurance card. As I got them from my bag, his flashlight traveled between my legs and he asked," Sir, are you wearing any clothes?"

"Well, actually, no." I said.

What else could I possibly say? I gave him the cards. He looked at them. He was very tall and very large. His rather nice-looking face was smiling. Handing me back the insurance card he asked, "Can you tell me why you're driving around naked?"

"Well, frankly, I just enjoy it."

He replied in a laugh, "Had anything to drink, Sir?"

"I had some beer earlier this evening."

"Would you object to a roadside breathalyzer test?"

I replied with a confident "No, Sir not at all."

He stepped away to his patrol car and returned with the disposable mouthpiece for the machine. I had laid aside the bag containing my clothes so now his view of my bare crotch was wide open. I followed his instructions, and he appeared satisfied that I wasn't over the legal limit.

He gave my license back and said "Hope you get into your house OK. Have a blanket or anything to put around yourself to get inside?"

"Not with me.", I said with an embarrassed expression on my face.

"Well, just be careful, I guess."

He smiled at me and waved me on. As I drove away, my heart was racing and my finger probed the wetness at the tip of my cock, a glance in the rear view mirror showed me what I expected.

The cop who spoke with me was talking with two other policemen. No doubt, they were hearing the whole story! It was as close as I've ever been to being arrested for public indecency. It was thrilling! I must applaud the policeman at the scene for being so open and amenable to my naked state. Who knows, perhaps he would like to have swapped places with me!

- Naked Carl

THE "BIG" OOPS!

Dear **NM**,

June 7, 1993 - I turned off the street into a parking lot on my way to the drug store for a few small items. Traveling thru the parking lot I headed for the back of the building to avoid traffic. Sitting there on the walk behind the building was a young guy having a sandwich and a soft drink. He looked like a workman from a construction company or something.

As I drove towards him he started to look around suspiciously as if he were about to do something he wasn't suppose to. Then he stood up and walked behind some sand bags. I don't know how he didn't see me, but he didn't! So i pulled ahead to see what he was about to do. Thats when I saw, to my surprise, he was taking off all of his clothes! I put on the brakes and stopped in the middle of the alley and watched as he laid down naked and started eating his lunch as if it were "normal" to do so! I just sat there staring at the sight of his balls laying on the concrete and the head of his cock laying on his balls.

He finally noticed me after several minutes because there was a loud skidding noise! I had been rolling in neutral the whole time and was pushing one of those plastic road barrels with my car. I was so embarrased. I looked at him as he gently covered up with his shorts, only to have his package fall out from underneath! He got so frustrated and embarrassed at me staring, he put his legs out infront of him to cover up. I mouthed "Oops" at him, as I drove on my way! I couldnt tell if he was mad at me or flattered or both!

-Embarrassed Allen from Fort Wayne, IN

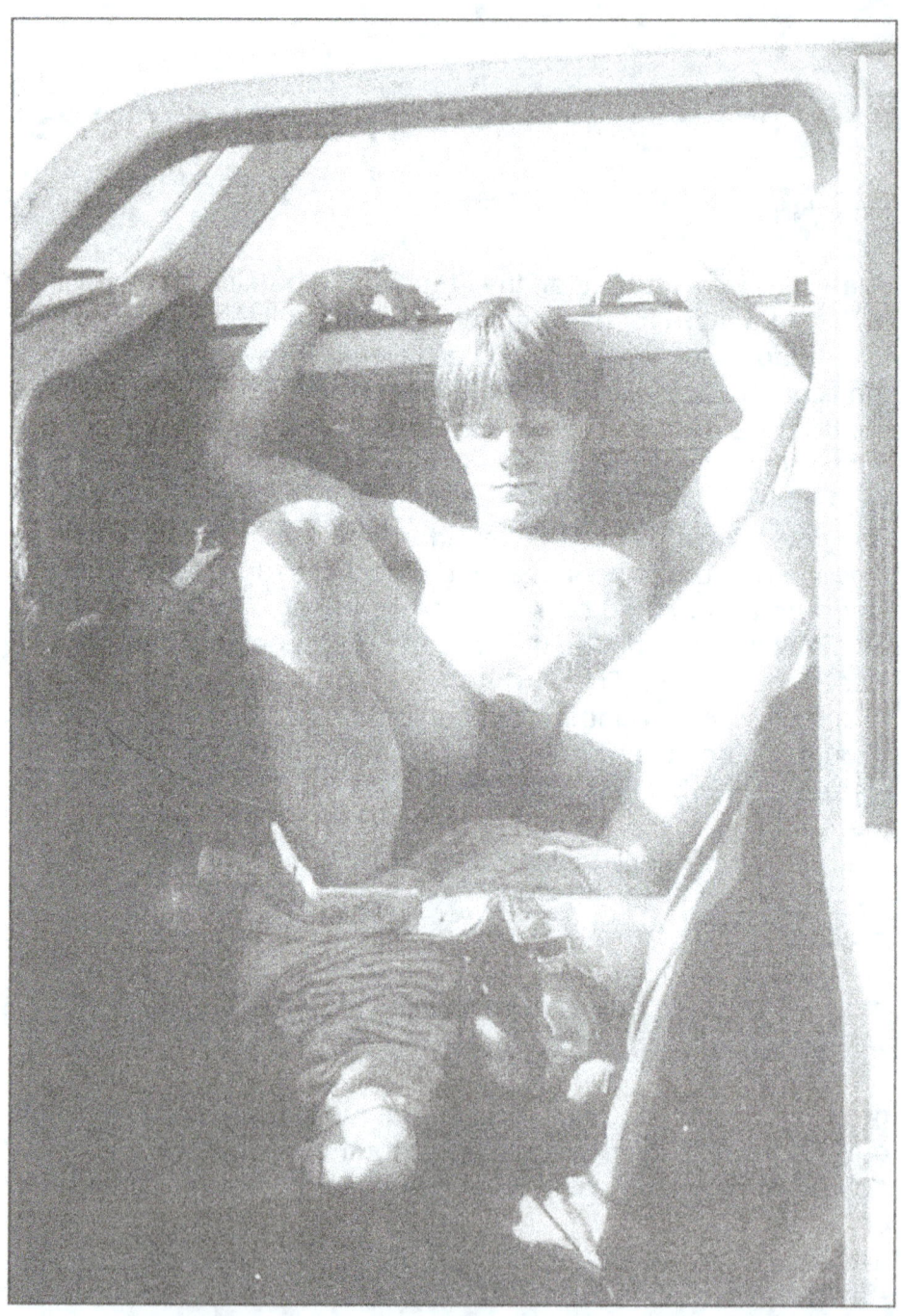

TRAFFIC JAM JACK-OFF

Dear **NAKED MAGAZINE**,

July 1996 - I got away from work about 4 o'clock, wanting to get home and continue working on a video I started the night before. I left the plant and was on 1-85 in a minute. I could stay in the right lane until my exit, about fifteen miles up the highway. I'd no sooner got up to speed than I saw the traffic jam in front of me. Typical, all lanes were stopped dead, and the cars stretched out as far as I could see ahead of me. I slammed on the brakes to a stop behind a panel van, a roll of carpet sticking out the back left door with the door tied with a piece of string to keep it from swinging open.

It was early July and the heat was a bitch. My air conditioner was on the blink, and I had both windows down in my S-10 pick-up, but sitting still in traffic was still awful. As I sat there, I noticed movement through the window of the closed door on the van in front of me. It was obviously the carpet crew who'd just finished a job, or were on their way to another job. All I could see was a silhouette. A couple of minutes later, the silhouette moved and the face of a hunk appeared at the window.

He was shirtless, had rugged features, and shoulder length brown hair. We immediately looked eye to eye. He smiled broadly. He moved to look out the open door, leaning with his right hand on the roll of carpet. His upper body was visible, and displayed a beautiful chest with an even tan. He didn't spend all his time indoors!

My fly was now open, and I was stroking myself just thinking about the guy. He held his pose for a moment, looking me in the eye. He then turned his head to say something to the driver. He stepped out of the van door and came toward me! He was wearing only a pair of cut-off shorts - very short and well-worn sneakers. He was just short of six feet tall, well shaped in every way, including the bulge in those shorts. He was too close and too fast for me to put my dick away, so I just let my right hand rest over it. I couldn't cover the fact that my fly was open, and even part of the shaft was still visible.

He was at my window in a flash. He asked me for a light for the cigarette he carried. I played hell getting my left hand into the pocket on the left side of my shirt, but wasn't about to move my right hand! I handed him the lighter and as he lit up, his gaze went to my lap. It took him a long time to light that cigarette!

He finally handed the lighter back to me, exhaling a deep drag of the smoke as he smiled and again our eyes met in total capture. "Why don't you pull up closer. No reason you can't get right up to the carpet roll, It won't hurt it. God knows, in this traffic we ain't going anywhere!" I eased my foot from the brake, rolling slowly towards the carpet. He kept his hand on my door, walking the few steps until I stopped again. I had no idea what difference this few feet could make, but I didn't question him.

"Great," he said as I stopped nearly touching the roll. He glanced one more time into my lap, giggled and went back to the van. He stepped up onto the carpet and once inside, turned and seated himself on the roll. I could see him sitting there straddling the roll, and realized that as close as I was to the van, and being in the right lane, probably no one else had the view I did! He groped himself with his free hand, forcing the shape of his dick to be visible in the fabric of his shorts. My own hand had gone back to stroking my cock, and I didn't try to hide the movements of my arm either! He moved and changed position until the opening of his shorts slipped back to reveal the engorged head of his cock!

From where I sat, it looked very large and red! Traffic inched along for a few minutes, but we couldn't have moved more than fifty feet. All this time, he continued to slowly move his hand up and down the hidden shaft while the head seemed to get bigger and redder! We jerked to a stop, again. He threw his left leg down on the carpet roll and raised his right foot nearly to his ass, pulling the leg of his shorts even further back and now exposing almost all of what had to be about 9" of very pretty, very straight, very hard meat!

With the leg of the shorts out of the way, the prick stood nearly straight up toward his stomach...as much as it could with the remaining strain of the shorts! I was about to explode! I didn't want to blow as long as the guy was doing this show, but God I was close! My left hand was absolutely wet with pre-cum.

Again, we moved slowly, probably another fifty feet. The guy finished his cigarette and flipped it out towards the shoulder of the road. He shifted and stood up, out of sight behind the closed door except for a silhouette. I thought the fun was over and was about to stroke myself to orgasm when he plopped back down on the roll of carpet. He'd taken off the shorts!

He was stark naked except for his sneakers! He sat there, in full view to me, his knees drawn up to his chest, arms on knees. I had an absolutely perfect view of his ponderous balls, which lay in a jiggling pile of the carpet, the 9+ inches of his meat pointing to his smiling face. He wiggled his fingers in a wave to me! Again, traffic edged forward slightly. I kept my right hand on my stiff prick, trying to hold off the pain I was feeling in my groin.

My eyes were glued to this naked hunk of a man that he was, sitting there smiling at me and moving slightly with the sway of the panel van. We soon stopped again. He leaned back on his elbows and spread his legs even further. The view now was heavy balls hanging on the carpet, covering what I suspected to be a beautiful asshole. What I could see of his cheeks were as brown and beautiful as the rest of his body. The guy was tanning nude somewhere!

His right hand grabbed hold of his cock, holding it by the base and leaving another handful exposed. His left hand came around and cupped his balls, then massaged them. He stroked slowly. He moved his feet into the air, resting one against the closed door and the other on the side of the open door. He moved his hand to his mouth, moistened his fingers and again moved that hand to lift his balls. The center finger found his asshole and started to slowly enter the pretty pucker. As his finger moved slowly in and out, he kept pace with his cock-stroking hand. I don't know how long this went on, I was totally lost in this blatant display of erotica on I-85 in North Atlanta!

He raised his head and looked out at me over the near-bursting cock. He pursed his lips and threw me a kiss as he plunged his fingers as deep into the hole as it would go, and made the final pull on his dick, shooting a stream of cum into the air. I counted three massive streams that looked three feet long as they left the slit of his dick. One of them landed on his stomach just beyond his pubic hair. Another hit the roll of carpet. I didn't know until later, after getting home, that one of the streams had landed on my front bumper!

There were other, smaller spurts and finally his hand stopped moving, holding his still hard cock just under the head, a large pool of white cream just resting there. We started moving again, very slowly as before. He sat up again, giving me another incredible smile, and shook the blob of jiz on his hand towards me. I made the final tug on my own bursting prick and felt the spray of my own cum hit me under the chin. I doubt that he could see that, but wish he could know how much I enjoyed what he'd done.

I looked down at my gray slacks and found them absolutely wet, and with many wet spots all over my legs. I raised my right hand and licked off my own juice, thinking it would have been nice to have tasted his gushing load. We continued to move slowly for quite a while. He just lay there for a few minutes.

Finally, he got up and again I saw the silhouette moving. I suppose he put the shorts back on. He went up front to sit in the passenger seat. I have no idea what, if anything, the guy driving might have seen of all this. I only know it's a firm memory that will never lose its ability to bring me to shooting my load across the room!

-Naked Brad

STRAIGHT BOY HORSE PLAY

Dear **Naked**,

July 22, 1994 - I am looking for a new place to live, and on my way to one of the houses, I saw three young guys walking down the street towards the river. They were wearing the long, loose shorts that are popular today. They started horsing around as I drove by. There was never any anger in their horsing around, it was just friendly play. But a little too friendly, so I decided to turn around and give a second look.

On my way back towards them I saw a little turn off, so I pulled over to where I could see them aproaching the river. And thats when all three of them ripped off there shorts and jump into the water. They splashed around for a bit, then the one guy jumped on the other guy and they both fell back into some mud and the three of them started wrestling around, knee deep in mud. I got so excited I have never seen anything like it. Three hot young men, laughing there asses off, while rubbing there bodies all over each other in the mud. Dicks and asses were flopping everywhere!

The one guy got pinned down and when he finally broke free and stood up he had a huge erection the other guys just pointed and laughed but when they both stood up they had hard-ons too. They all three just stood there laughing at each other, then dove back into the deeper end and washed off. I quickly jacked myself off as they were making their way back to there shorts. Such a disapointment, three hot guys with no gay ambitions, at least I got some good eye candy to help me jack off for a while.

-naked Rob

PEEPING GLEN

Dear **NM**,

Trying to remember experiences for your magazine, I remembered my first college year in 1975. In the men's dorm there was this one guy who didn't wear clothes much. He liked to sit naked in the hall, just outside his room, studying or talking with other guys. He had shoulder length, light brown hair, a nice face and a really good body. I never met him - actually I was afraid to meet him because I didn't want other guys to think I was interested in him.

Besides, at that age there was still the involuntary hard-on that might have embarrassed me. Still, I would always try to find a reason to pass him or go out to the hall when I knew he was there. I wish I would have had the courage to meet him and join him. I might have actually joined him if I didn't have high school friends there in the dorm with me.

The reaction from the other guys, as far as I could tell, was basically "so what". He was totally accepted and I never heard anyone say anything negative about him. If I had the chance to experience that time again with what I know now, I would definitely make the effort to meet him and join him in hanging out naked. It would have been very liberating and something that would have been very good for me at that time.

I would love to hear from other guy's experiences of nudity in the dorms. I had to move to a new apartment because of the January quake. That was a hassle. Anyway, one night there was some guy on a motorcycle going up and down the street over and over again. His motorcycle sounded like it didn't have a muffler (if they have one or not I don't know). It was irritating and I went out on my porch to see who it was. I noticed I wasn't the only one irritated since there was many people at their doors trying to see who was making all that noise.

Well the guy drove off shortly after I stepped outside. Just as I was stepping back in, something caught my eye. There was this guy on his balcony naked wearing only bed-slippers checking out the source of the noise. I tried to see if I could get a better look but I didn't have binoculars or anything that would help me get a better look. I decided to buy some binoculars which I did the next day.

That afternoon, when I got home, I went to my window put my new binoculars up to my eyes in the direction of that guy in his slippers and saw nothing but closed blinds. I decided to scope out the rest of the neighborhood and the first thing I see is this guy walking naked out of his first story apartment over to a stream just behind the side of his building. He must have had company there because he looked like he was talking to someone on his porch. He also would dance a little like he was pretending to be a stripper. This went on for about ten minutes until he went back into his apartment and then came back out in his underwear and a drink in his hand. He spent some more time seemingly talking to someone then went back inside. He must of been about thirty-five with a relatively good body. I waited for several more minutes with my cock pointing straight up, but he didnt come back out, so I got bored and went inside and jacked off a huge load across my chest with the help of the visions of his ass dancing around the yard.

Since then, I haven't seen him naked again...yet!

-Naked Zach, College Station, TX

DRUNKEN FRENCH

Dear **NAKED MAGAZINE**,

When I used to go to Venice beach in the mid-eighties, there was always the opportunity to see some male nudity in public. Guys swimming in the ocean would frequently take off their swimsuits and wear them over their shoulders or wrap them around their wrists and play in the ocean naked. You'd always get to see their ass or penis when the waves would dip below their waists or when the guys would jump into a wave. I did it myself!

Frequently I'd see guys arrive to the beach, spread out their blanket or towel, sit and remove their clothes. They would not have a swimsuit on underneath but have to get completely naked only for an instant before they put on the swimsuit.

One memorable event happened when a very cute, very drunk young French guy decided that he didn't want to wear a swimsuit. I am presuming he decided that since I don't really know why he was naked when I looked up and saw him. He was just standing there really doing nothing but rambling in a French accent.

A lifeguard went over to get him to cover up, which he did. As the lifeguard turned to leave he dropped the shorts again. When the lifeguard returned, the guy said that they weren't his shorts. I saw someone throw a swimsuit at him and he put it on.

The lifeguard left again. I didn't see the French guy nude again that day but it was a nice show while it lasted. It would have been a really nice show if the guy wouldn't have been so drunk. But it was innocent and the lifeguard knew it. Basically, the French guy was doing what was natural to him since the French are used to seeing nudity or being naked on their beaches.

-Naked John

SHIRTLESS

Dear **Naked Magazine**,

One night while cruising in the Griffith Park area, I noticed a guy driving around without a shirt. Nothing unusual except that it was a rather chilly evening. Actually, you can see many guys driving around without their shirts on. Its always turned me on because I imagine that they are driving nude. A little later, I noticed his car parked near another car. After a couple of minutes, I noticed that his door was open. The car he was near also had its door open.

It was very dark and hard to see. I finally noticed that the guy was standing with another guy between both cars. I could barely tell that they were both naked. I guess they were jerking off for each other. They would get back in their cars whenever another car drove up to turn.

It ended when a park ranger was coming down the road, you can tell it's them because they shine lights into cars and bushes. The guy drove off quickly so he would not be seen or caught. That's all I have seen so far but I look for him whenever I go there hoping to finally show him that I share in his fantasy-fulfillment of driving around naked.

-Naked Roy

NEW TO NUDITY

Dear **Naked**,

When I was younger and naive and before I became what you would call a nudist, I knew I was interested in nudity. I remember a friend who had no trouble hanging around his house nude. I was not use to it then and didn't really spend my time at home naked, even though I wanted to. One time after a nice episode of sex, He invited me into the kitchen to get a drink. We were sitting there at the kitchen table when the kitchen doorbell rang. My immediate impulse was to run and hide but I decided I might look silly doing it in front of him.

He got up and went to the door like he was very used to it, which he probably was. This rather nice-looking neighbor came in. They started talking about something I don't remember now. My friend invited the guy to sit and have a drink, which he did. So there we were, two naked guys and a fully-clothed guy sitting around a kitchen table talking. At first I was uncomfortable about it because I had never experienced something like this before.

The guy stayed for quite sometime talking. I would frequently catch myself looking at the two of them, seeing how it really didn't matter at all whether one was nude while the other was not. The situation would sometimes start to turn me on. I didn't want to become erect in front of this stranger, so I thought of other things quickly.

I began to enjoy the feeling of not having to be ashamed or not having to automatically cover up my nudity. The guy would look but it was never intrusive. He must have been used to coming over and hanging out with my nudist friend. After a while, I wondered if he ever got naked here with my friend.

The guy finally left and I asked my friend about him. What does he think of your unashamed nakedness in front of him? Did he ever join him? My friend said that the guy was used to it because he was sort of a nudist, as well. He would join him and spend his evening naked with my friend, watching a video or the TV. He also volunteered the information that their evenings together were always non-sexual. I thought that was really cool. I have since turned on guys to spending a nice evening together naked. Sometimes non-sexually, but mostly we would have to get past that point.

Many times, my guest would begin to put something on after our encounter. I would encourage him to stay naked and relax. Of course, any time we'd get together again, he would be more inclined to stay naked. Soon it was the most natural thing for a guy to come over, strip as he got in the door and hang out with me. I liked it and they did, too. Most of my friends are more than willing to get naked with me. It's still fun to get a new friend used to it. Most get into it, some don't, but I'll always keep trying.

- Naked Richard

MY FIRST SKINNY DIP

Dear **NM**,

I remember a time when I went on a hike with my friend Jack. We liked to go up into the mountains to a little valley with a small pond in it. We never went into the water, though. On one hike when we were just about there, I heard noises of splashing water. We both figured that someone was already there. We quietly wanted to see who it was so we snuck up to take a look.

There was this long-haired guy in the water. We couldn't see anyone else. He didn't talk to anyone so we guessed he was alone. He swam about for a while. I asked Jack why we never went swimming there and he just shrugged. We watched as the guy finally climbed out. We were surprised to see that he was naked. Jack had to stifle a snicker. I thought it was a turn-on. This guy was rather handsome with a nice body. We could tell he was older than us. We were around 18. He was about 26 or so. He went to a blanket and laid down on it face up. Soon, Jack asked if we were going to hide here and watch him all day or what. I asked him what we should do. Jack said either leave or do what we always do, that being, sitting on the shore relaxing, exploring the area, or just hanging out here.

We finally decided that we came all this way, and we didn't want to have done it for nothing. We decided to do what we were here for. We started walking towards the guy. He heard us and looked up. He sat up and watched us but did not make any attempt to cover up. We didn't really look at him much but as we got closer he said "Hi!" We said hi and sat down under the tree near him. We found out his name was Russell.

As we talked he asked if we were offended by his nudity. Jack and I had to think about it and decided that it didn't bother us. After some more talk, Jack asked him how the water was. He said it was great and that we should go in. We hesitated and the talk went on to other subjects. Finally, Russell said he was going in the water again. We watched him swim for a while. Russell started encouraging us to go into the water. Jack suddenly said he would and began to undress.

I watched him as he got naked and climbed in. I had never seen Jack completely naked before. All the while he was telling me to join him. I watched them swim around some and decided to go in, too. I took off all my clothes and went in. It was cold at first but easy to get used to. We did a lot of horse play and grab ass and it was really fun. Soon we got tired and got out to rest. Jack asked Russell if he always went naked in the mountains. Russell said it was the way he liked to be in nature the best. Then he said he spends his time at home nude, too. Both Jack and I mentioned that it was hard to hang out naked at home but that sometimes we slept naked. That was something I didn't know about Jack before. Russell said that when we got places of our own we could do what ever we wanted to, including not wearing clothes.

He told us a lot of things that day about nudity and I have to admit that I agreed with everything he said. We spent the rest of the day there naked with Russell. We all left together and when we split, he told us where he was from and that we were invited to visit him whenever we were in that area. We did visit him but that's another story for another time.

- Naked Doug

ARRESTED WHILE DRIVING NAKED

Dear **NM**,

Here's a story of "arrested while driving naked" in August of 1989 on a very hot night. My boyfriend and I were leaving a bar in Washington, D.C. We had both driven in separate cars. I was in one of my get naked moods, so I came up with the idea of driving home in the buff. To make it more interesting, I put my clothes in my boyfriend's car.

We left at the same time, but he left me behind really fast. I did not want to draw any attention to myself because of the naked situation that I was in. The drive should have only taken about a half-hour, but I was badly mistaken. After about ten minutes, I realized that I had had one too many drinks. So I pulled over to the side of the road to sober up.

Forty-five minutes later, and feeling a little better, I was about to leave when I noticed a pair of headlights approaching the rear of my car. My heart started pounding like a drum. As I looked into the rear view mirror, I could see the shape of a man walking towards my side window. I was freaked out, I didn't want anyone to catch me this way. He tapped on the window, I looked up only to become sick to my stomach. All my fears about being naked came true. I was eye to eye with a state trooper.

He asked me for some identification and why I was nude. I told him that I was doing this on a bet and that my ID was in another car. He had me get out and walk a straight line right there on the side of the road. There were a few cars passing by that slowed down. I guess they thought that they were seeing things. Which they were, EVERYTHING! I failed the test and he handcuffed me and put me in his cruiser. The really weird thing was that I really did not seem to mind. In all reality, it was sort of a turn on. The best part about it was the fact that I got to be naked in public. I no longer drink and drive but I go naked every chance I get.

-Steven Staying Naked

MYSTERIOUS IN THE DARK

Dear **NM**,

This Experience happened recently. Wait till you hear it! I was dropping off a new friend after a date. I did not drive off right away but wanted to rest a bit and think about this guy. I liked him. I backed up out of sight of his house so he couldn't see that I was still there. The street was dark and it was very late - about three in the morning. A few minutes later, I noticed a bit of movement in front of his house.

Thinking he saw me and was coming out to see why I was still there, I was about to get out of the car to greet him, but I hesitated. The figure did not get closer to me. I decided to see what he was doing. Finally he started walking down the sidewalk in my direction. As he got closer, I am surprised to see that the figure was completely naked. It sort of looks like my new friend but I am not really sure. It has to be him, no one else lives there.

I'm turned on because the guy is erect and stroking it. He didn't see me because of the darkness. I see him continue walking down about three houses. All these things go through my head. Part of me says to stay still and never say anything about it. The other part of me wants to join him. I don't want to jump out and scare him, so I stay still and continue to watch. By now, I'm hard in my pants and I have to adjust myself.

I look away from him for a while to "fix" myself and when I look back, I don't see him anymore. I look all around but I can't find him. I rolled down my window to get a better look but still see nothing around. The darkness doesn't help either. After a couple of minutes, I'm startled by something moving across the street on the sidewalk. The figure stops and faces my direction. I now know that he knows I'm there.

I can't make out the guy's face but I'm still barely able to see that he's naked and stroking a hard-on. I don't know what to do so I sit and watch him for what seems like an eternity. Finally, I think I hear a whisper. I listen more closely and I hear, "Get out of your car." Because I don't know who it is, I'm feeling a little wary about getting out. I hope it's the guy I just dropped off. From what I can see, he's got a great body. I hear him say it again.

Finally, I open the door and step outside my car. At that moment, I'm semi-hard. I'm a bit afraid but still turned-on by what's happening. Now I hear the guy whisper, "Take off your shirt." I take off my t-shirt and my dick gets a little harder. I find that I am enjoying this. After a pause, I decide to remove my shoes and socks without him telling me to. I then begin to unbutton my jeans and pull them down. I am not wearing any underwear. As I do this, I hear him whisper, "Yeah!" There I am now, naked and erect on this dark, residential street with another naked erect guy who I think I know. "Play with it." I hear now. I do. I want to know who this is, so I begin to walk towards the guy.

I hear him whisper, "No, stay there!" I back up. I can kind of see him bend his knees as he leans back a bit while stroking it. He's doing it for me. I begin to do the same for him. Again I hear, "Yeah!", in a muffled whisper. Obviously, he's into exhibitionism and voyeurism, anonymous exhibitionism and voyeurism. He turns around and bends down to show me his ass. Even though it's very dark, I can still make out a great-looking ass. I do the same for him. I'm getting pretty close now with the excitement of this situation. After a time of showing off, I whisper to him that I'm close. "Shoot it!', I hear him whisper back.

As I get closer to cumming, I notice that he's getting a

little closer to me. I try to see if I can make out his face better but he begins to cum and I get caught up in the moment and watch him shoot as I also shoot. I'm one who can barely stand up when I cum, so I jerk and spasm for a while. When I regain myself, I look to the guy who is now back across the street. I hear him whisper, "Thanks!" and he begins to walk. I whisper for him to, "Wait!" And it seemed to make him start running away from me quicker.

I watch as the figure runs down the sidewalk, still naked. I hear the sound of his bare feet hitting the pavement. I begin to put on my clothes when I realize he did not run towards the house my friend lives in. The thoughts run through my mind that it was either a stranger or my friend wants to make me think it wasn't him by running away from his house.

After I'm dressed and in my car, I decide to drive around the corner and sneak back to see if the figure comes back to my friends house. Then, I'll know. I hide in the bushes near my friend's house for a while but nobody shows up. Soon, I begin to feel stupid waiting there and head on home feeling surprisingly good.

The next few times I saw my friend, he said nothing to indicate he was the guy. I have thrown hints at him but he doesn't respond like he knows. I have since seen my friend naked. He has a great ass but I'm still not sure it was him but it probably wasn't. Whoever it was though, I really enjoyed showing off and being naked outside, and he put on a great show. I also enjoyed doing it for him, as well. It really turned me on to see someone naked like that and it turns me on to know that I did it, too. I am going to go back there soon, late at night, to see if the same thing happens again. If it does, I'll try to see who it really is and I'll let you know.

-Curiously Naked in Phoenix

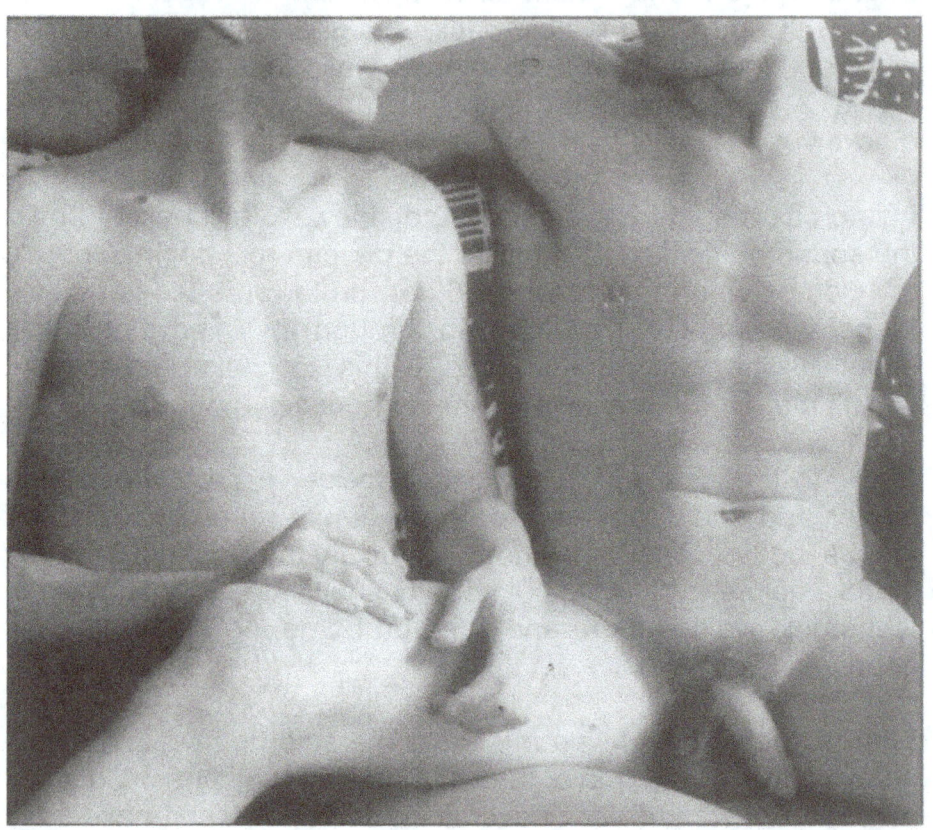

SEXY STRAIGHT SECRETS

DEAR **NAKED MAGAZINE,**

Here in town, there's a "straight" porno theatre but it's frequented by switch-hitters, kinky couples, college students, truck drivers and lots of gays and bisexuals, and these days, who isn't one of these. I go in spurts because it's kind of expensive and the videos are lousy. But the occasional memorable experience keeps me coming. I've had about half a dozen mind blowing experiences there and here's one of them.

Before reading any further strip down or at least pull your pants down. Hey, I'm writing naked so you should read naked! - One day last summer I went to the theatre straight from school and boy was I horny. After paying my money and waiting for my eyes to adjust to the darkness, I found a seat down front towards the screen. After a while I noticed a handsome dude with a handle-bar mustache and a reversed baseball cap in the row in front of me slightly to the left.

He looked very straight and so I felt nervous masturbating or even unzipping my fly within his earshot. After about ten minutes, I said what the heck and unzipped. To be safe, I covered my lap with the sweater I had in my backpack. It felt good hand-humping near this dude. Within minutes I saw him glance back real quickly and I sensed he knew what I was doing and it didn't look like he minded. So I kept it up (so to speak). After he looked back again, I leaned forward and saw that this guy was bare-ass naked except for his hat, watch, shoes, socks and a horny grin!

I kept looking and he got off on it. I have seen nudity in this theatre before but it is rare and usually guys only pull their pants down half-way at most. So this guy was in naked heat and was loving showing off. Luckily it's pretty dark there but the illumination from the screen told me he was one horny dog. He was tanned, stocky, in good shape, about 30 and he had a mischievous grin that would make even the most shy guy crave to get naked and nasty.

About now, he motioned me to come into his row with several swings of his head, and a masculine smile. When I got closer, I could vaguely see a pile of clothes on the floor and I sat with a chair in between us empty because I was a little nervous and I wanted him to have some space. Also, we'd look less suspicious if anyone were watching us. He leaned over the empty seat and whispered in my ear that he'd love to jack off with me and see me naked. Before I could respond fully, he shifted into the seat next to me (I caught a glimpse of his white ass, huge balls and thick dick) and he started unbuttoning my shirt. I gave up and let this nude dude go for it.

Off came my shirt, then he unbuckled my pants, unzipped them, and worked them down my legs. When they got stuck at my shoes, he slipped those off, too. Now all I had on was my socks, underwear and undershirt. He got on the pile of clothes on the floor and stripped off my boxer shorts and slowly took off each sock. I kept my undershirt on and really got off on being "butt" naked with this guy. Minutes later we both got off. Afterwards, he told me he was married with four kids, and that he digs getting naked with guys and "waxing the dolphin". I can't say that I blame him.

-Robert Hunter

RAVE PARTY

DEAR **NAKED**,

A couple of summers ago a friend invited me to go with him to this gathering called The Big Bang. It was actually a rave (underground party) with a live band. It was held in an old automotive shop yard. There were a lot of different types of people there, men and women. It was a very alternative-type crowd. The band was very different also. They would burn stuffed toy animals as part of their act, among other strange happenings.

I am bringing this up because a couple of band members got naked or near naked with genitals showing during their time on stage. It was actually a lot of fun. There were also a couple guys in the crowd who took off their clothes except for a hat and their sport shoes and just walked around like everyone else seeing what there was to be seen.

Another guy I saw there wore a large t-shirt and sport shoes and that was all. He had great legs and every once in a while someone would lift his t-shirt and a nice butt or a fine set of balls would be seen underneath. I was really tempted to take off my clothes, too, but then the police came and closed the party for being too loud. No nudity-related arrests were made but I was glad I didn't join in. But I will if I ever go back to another one of those kinds of parties.

-Naked-Lover Roy from N. Hollywood

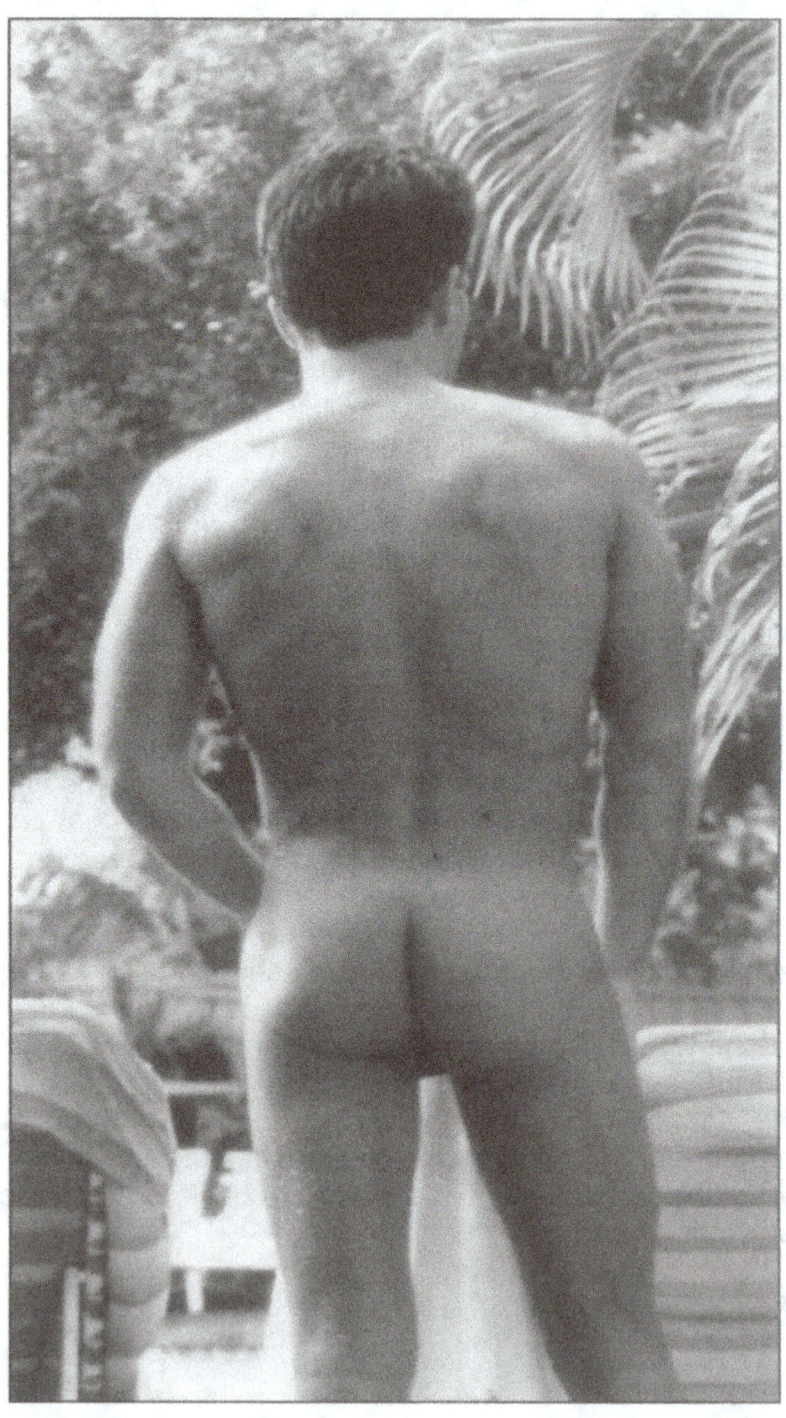

FANTASY FULFILLED

DEAR **NAKED**,

Some time ago, when I was just beginning to go to the bars, I had a fun experience that, I think, you would like to hear about. I met this good looking guy and we hit it off well. He invited me over to his house. I said I would follow him but he said that he would drive me back. As we're talking on the way to his apartment, he asked me what a fantasy of mine would be. I thought about it for a while, or so I wanted him to think, then said that I like to drive naked with someone. This was something I did fantasize about but actually never did.

He pulled to the sidewalk suddenly. I thought he got mad or something, but he started to take off his shirt. I watched him as I felt my heart start to pound. He said I should take off my clothes too. I did so while I watched him take everything completely off. In a short while, I was also completely naked and he began driving again. It was exhilarating and very much a turn-on for me to be with him like this. I was hard in a minute and he was getting there. I liked what I saw when I looked at him but I still wanted to see if anyone might see us, so I didn't watch him all the time.

After to short a time, he turned into a driveway and waited as the garage door opened into the underground parking of an apartment building. It was about 2 AM now. He parked and we got out. I was starting to put my clothes back on when he asked me why I was doing that. I didn't answer as I watched him pick up his clothes and head for the elevator. I did the same. It was tense right after he pressed the button before the door opened. Luckily no one was there. We got in and he pressed three, the top floor. Again, I got very nervous as we waited for the door to re-open. Again no one was there. He stepped out and I followed him. I watched him walk very comfortably to his apartment which, by the way, was the furthest one from the elevator. It was a large courtyard-type building so anyone on the walkways could see us. I don't think anyone did. Finally at his front door, we go in.

After a glass of water and a piss. He brings out two towels and says to follow him. Holding the towel if front of him, he goes out the front door. I follow holding my towel in my hand as well. We seem to be going back to the elevator. We hear a noise from beneath us and we both put the towel around our hips. We continue past the elevator and then up some stairs to the roof. There we laid the towels down and finally had some of the hottest sex I have ever had! It was great! I had never done anything like that before.

When we were done, we wore the towels back to his apartment. We both got dressed and he drove me back to my car. I never saw him again. I wish I had gotten a number but I didn't. Maybe he's reading this now. If so, thanks for fulfilling, no, surpassing my fantasy. I will always remember this encounter.

- Richard

LUCKY

DEAR **NAKED MAGAZINE,**

I like the experiences that people send in and I have a strange one that, even though it happened very quickly, you might be able to use. I had to return a tape that I had rented and since I lived pretty close, I walked. After returning it, I decided to take another way home. As I was walking, I looked over to a building across the street. I saw a shirtless guy in an upper story, open window. I stopped to watch him. He was bending out to look down to the sidewalk. As I watched, he lifted himself up on his arms to get a better look down. No one was down there, by the way. As he got higher, I saw that he seemed to not be wearing anything else either. In fact, I saw his pubes and the upper half of his enormous cock.

While I was standing there, I noticed a truck passing slowly (because of traffic.) I looked in and saw a guy looking at me. I glanced down his body and he was also naked. I looked at his face again and he smiled. I looked back to the window. That guy was no longer there. I looked back at the guy in the truck. He had to move forward now because the traffic was now moving. I followed him but as I caught up to him he went further. Then the traffic started moving again and off he went. That night I had a great time jerking off thinking about these two naked guys. I was at the right place at the right time.

-Lucky Voyeur

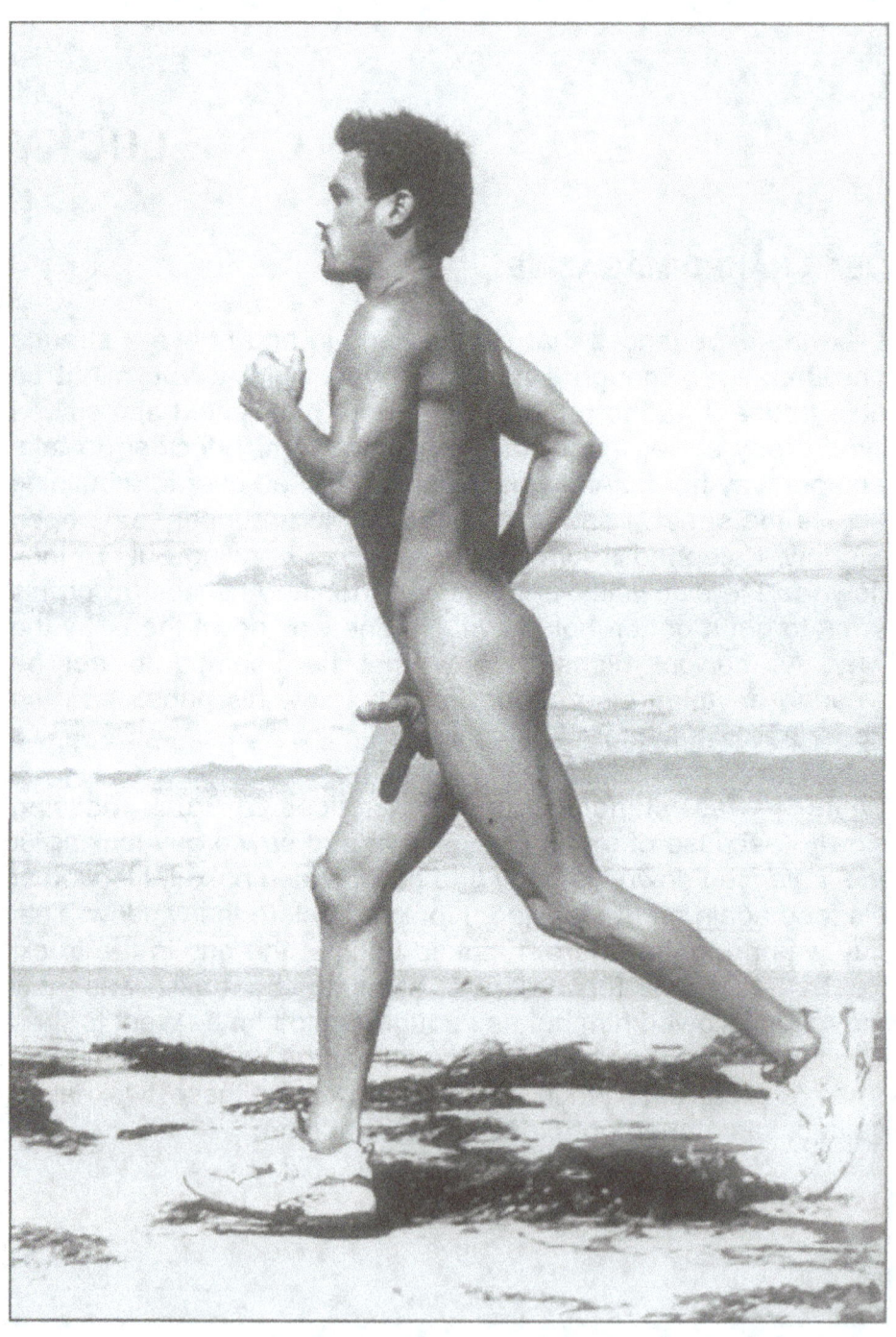

A QUICK FREE SHOW

DEAR **NAKED**,

I live near a cruisy area here in North Hollywood. Sometimes I go out walking that area to see who's driving around. One night recently I had just gotten back from a walk and decided to sit on the steps leading up to my apartment. I could see a guy squatting down against a wall up the street. While I sat there watching him and the cars go around and around. All of a sudden, I saw a guy run across the street and he wasn't wearing anything, he was completely naked! He was carrying something which I presume were his clothes. He came around the corner and almost ran over the squatting guy, who sprung up quickly.

The naked runner veered away from him and dashed across the street, out of view. I continued to watch the previously squatting guy watch the runner. It was over, the guy resumed the squatting position and soon I went inside and went to bed. That was it, but I was glad to have witnessed it.

-Rudy from N. Hollywood

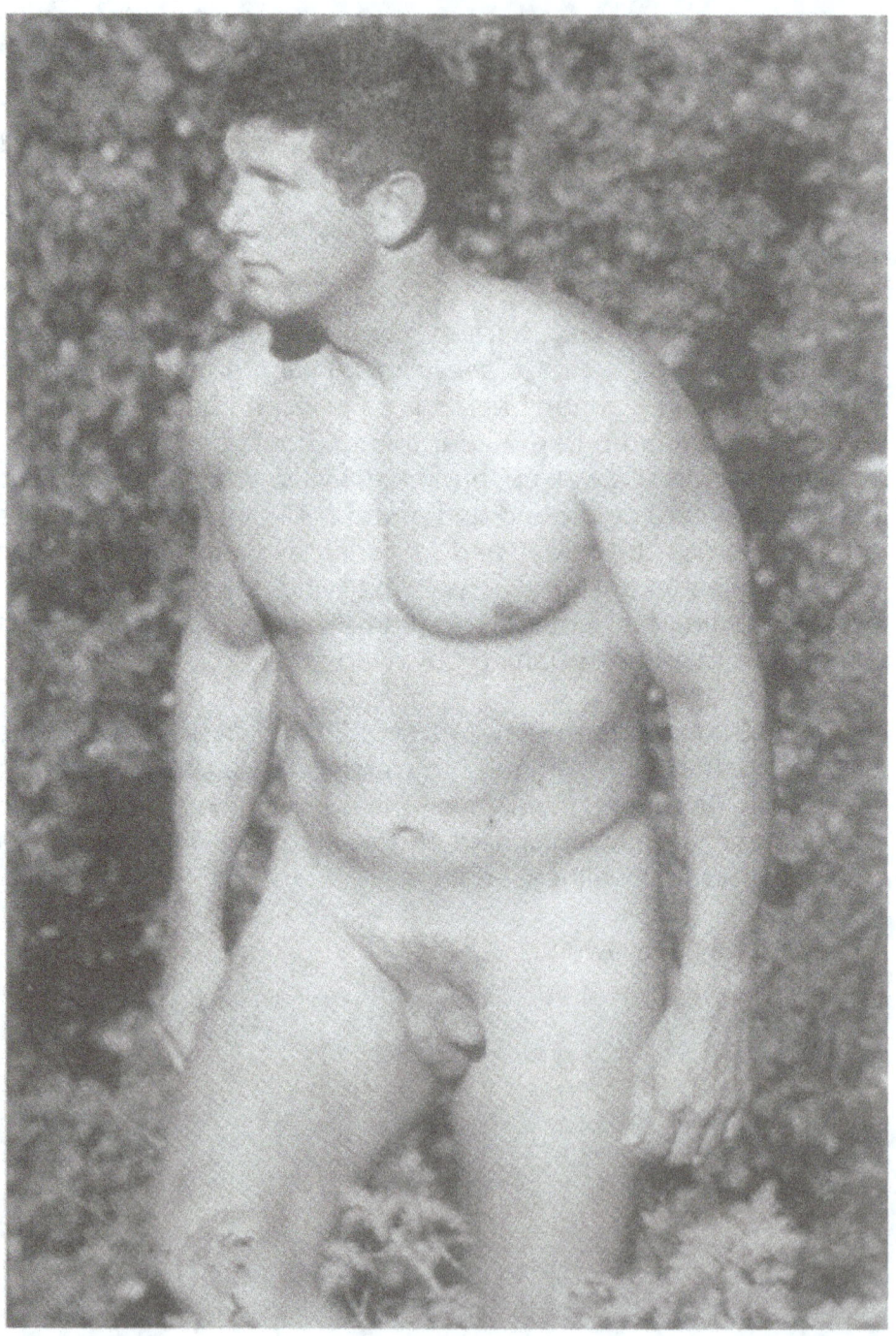

NATURE BOY

DEAR **NM**,

Anyone familiar with gay Los Angeles knows that Griffith Park has a long and hallowed history of cruisy bushes, trails and roads, of horny guys and undercover cops setting traps. But a few years ago, the road that had long been the primary cruising stretch was closed down, presumably because of road damage. As a result, the road has been practically deserted, except for occasional hikers and bike riders. In this nature boy's opinion, it's also become more fun and adventuresome without the constant traffic of professional cruisers driving back and forth all day.

So I often go for late afternoon hikes or mountain bike rides. Sometimes when that certain spirit motivates me (you know the one) I find myself just ripping off whatever clothes I'm wearing and making my trip totally naked, or at least pulling my balls out of my shorts and letting them enjoy the breeze and view as I climb the road. And then comes the drama of just how brazen I will become should other people happen to come my way. But one occasion stands out above all others.

One hot summer afternoon at sunset I started up the road for a hike, and soon noticed two other guys heading up the same way about 50 yards behind me. It was one of those sultry afternoons when all I wanted to do was rip off my shorts, but I found myself a bit intimidated by the presence of these guys just behind me. To my surprise, however, just when wearing anything was about to drive me crazy, I looked over my shoulder to see both the guys had stopped and were ripping off all their clothes!

Needless to say, I needed no more encouragement and off came the shorts.

Now there were the three of us hiking naked up the road, still separated by the same distance. Of course, any other hikers or a ranger could have come by, but the hot hazy dusk air absorbed any such concerns. The pair of guys took off on a side trail. Soon another hiker was coming down, a rather hot looking Latin man, but I made no move to cover myself, and as he passed me he stopped, got this wild look in his eye and strode right up to me. He grabbed my dick, pulled his out, and jacked off and sprayed his cum almost immediately!

He then composed himself and continued down the road, leaving me stunned and only further charged by the encounter. So I proceeded ahead, where a short time later another hiker had stopped to enjoy the view. I too stopped at the viewpoint, curious to see what he'd do. But this one was shy, continually staring at my brazenness, making those little subconsciously controlled gestures that showed he wanted it, but making no move. This was almost hotter than the previous guy, just knowing that I was driving him crazy but nothing happening.

The standoff continued for quite a while, until finally he moved off and went down the road. Of course, I wasn't at all disappointed. I was just on fire! By now it was getting dark and I was quite a ways up the mountain, so I took a trail down that just happened to conveniently go by the traditional cruising area. How far could I go without putting my clothes on? I decided to stay at the edge of the area. After all, I was more into just being naked out there than playing any cruising games or encountering an undercover cop. But sure enough, as soon as I got down to the road that would have any traffic on it, there was some guy almost on cue, waiting behind a tree for me. He dropped to his knees and started working on me, but soon I heard the noise of people approaching on the trail, so I panicked and put on my shorts.

Well, if it wasn't the two naked hikers I'd left long ago, now returning and still happily nude! Of course I ripped my shorts off again, embarrassed at having clothed myself so unnecessarily (how's that for a reversal of the usual situation!). My attentions immediately shifted from the guy who'd been working his mouth on me to my naked compatriots, and I joined them for the remaining walk back to our cars.

The energy between these naked conspirators was intense, but it was more about the act of being nude than about sex. Lingering at our cars, we talked about going on another naked hike, but of course I lost the number and it hasn't happened. But I'll bet they subscribe to NAKED and are reading this right now!

-C.C. from Los Angeles

COWBOY CROTCH!

DEAR **NAKED**,

Here's a cute happening that I have to tell your reader's about. I went to my uncles ranch about a year ago to help with the round up. It was a hot sweaty stinky day. There were three of us out there on horses and in front of us on a four wheeler was this very cute young man named Chad he must have been about 21 years old. He was shirtless and wore only a pair of loose-fitting, torn jeans, and some cowboy boots. My uncle told Chad and I to go down the one side of the mountain and we would meet up on the other side.

Chad and I started down the side of the mountain together and we came upon a barb-wire fence and as I leaned over to open the fence I slipped and fell off my horse, I wasnt hurt just my jeans were torn and caught on the fence. Chad came around and I guess he didn't know exactly how loose his jeans were because as he plunged his hand into his pocket to get his knife his jeans went down too! He turned towards me, I got to see his pubes and his dick because he wasn't wearing any underwear. He was truly a light brown brunette all over. He didnt even take the time to bring them back up as he was more worried about my leg. He just started sawing at my jeans as his pants fell lower and lower to the ground. And to my surprise his dick grew bigger and bigger. Just as my jaw was about to hit my chest he said "all done" and pulled his pants back up.

I replayed that scene over and over in my head for weeks!

-Tim from Santa Fe, NM

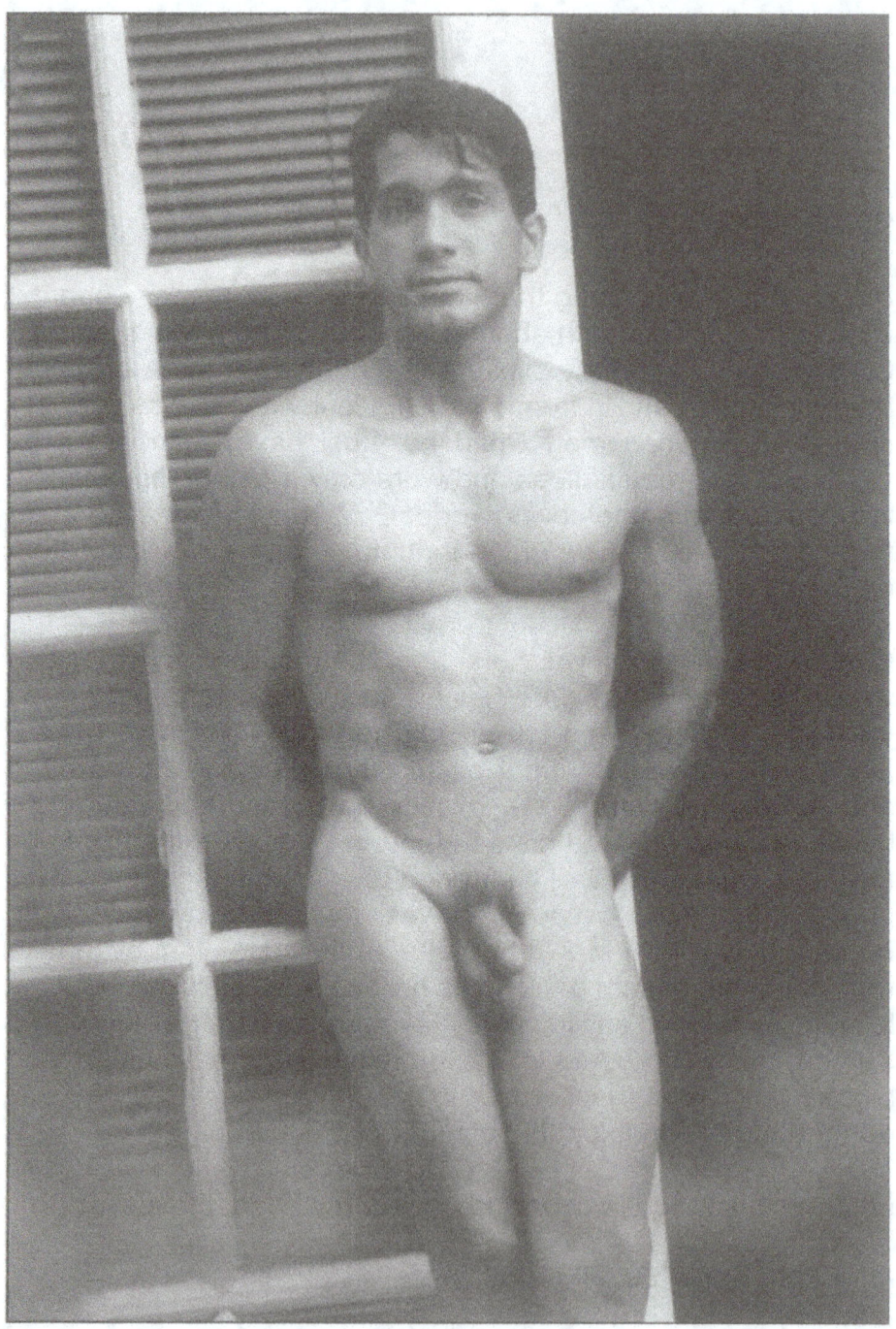

BILLY AT THE LAUNDROMAT

DEAR **NAKED MAGAZINE,**

I really enjoy your magazine, especially the "Experiences" section. I have one that happened just last Saturday - October 1,1994. I went to do some laundry at a Laundromat right in the middle of West Hollywood. There always seems to be some cruising going on there and I began checking out some guys.

This one good-looking guy was wearing some very short denim-type shorts. We would look at each other every so often. He was also checking out a couple of other guys as well. He was at the other end of the Laundromat for a while but then came to sit near me. He was at the end of the center aisle between the washing machines. I soon noticed that another guy seemed to keep looking at this guy's crotch. I soon saw what the other guy was looking at.

The guy near me was sitting in a position so that his dick and balls could be seen up his shorts. Actually, all he had to do was to open his legs and there they were. I soon had to check on my laundry, twice, which was right in the view line of his crotch, and of course, he let me look up his shorts, too.

It was a very nice view and when I looked at his face, he would be smiling at me. I was also wearing short shorts but they were made of material that snug close to my legs and wouldn't offer others a view. Anyways we did get to talking and I gave him my number. He called, but as of this writing, we haven't gotten together. Next time I do laundry, I'll be wearing the right shorts!

- Billy from West Hollywood

A PIECE OF HEAVEN

DEAR **NAKED MAGAZINE**,

I love your magazine because it is both, informative, as well as imaginative. I had to write to tell everyone about a weekend every reader should have. I went to Palm Springs for the recent Labor Day weekend for a little R&R and got anything but. A friend of mine told me about this really cool hotel where you can sunbathe in the nude, but it's what he didn't tell me that really kept me "up" all weekend.

I checked in and found a tropical paradise that was anything but "desert"-like. There were flowers, bird sounds, music, sun and the most beautiful, chiseled, and statuesque men with perfect pecs and haircuts. They smiled revealing the most perfect teeth. And they were just the pool boys. The hot tub was big enough to seat 30, but it wasn't your tradition all around shape, rather it was in the design of a snake as it hid itself among the trees whose branches and vines fell over the steaming waters.

Here was lot's to spy on. Even though it was about 110 degrees outside, we never felt it because the little spray misters kept everything tropically moist and cool. After I checked into my room, complete with Jacuzzi tub set in a glass alcove over-looking the antics of the garden, I took off all my clothes and ventured outside. At first I felt very naked as I walked through the lobby and into the bar, but everyone else was naked and rum has a way of making everything all right.

Paying for drinks is not a problem and there's no need to carry cash, since everything is billed to your room. My bartender's name was Michael. I'll never forget him. He was dressed only in a black leather g-string and had a tanned stomach which almost took my focus away from the gaze of his steely blue eyes. This man had eyelashes for days.

As I sat down he asked me my name and told me how handsome I was. This was a man who "knew" his work. I said "Thank you" and returned the compliment. He served me my drink and smiled. I started to get excited as he handed my glass to me and I was so glad to be hidden by the bar at that moment, but he knew. It was just one of those moments.

Soon, I was comfortable and feeling the need to venture out into the garden and check out the scenery. The first few things that caught my attention was the banana trees, the sound of the waterfalls and Ella Fitzgerald in the background. The sun was great, I was smiling and feeling good. I came upon the first lagoon and waded in. The water was cool and sweet.

As I turned the corner, from around a huge rock, I saw this guy, he couldn't have been over twenty-three, leaning back on the rock, his head tilted back enough so that his Adams apple was slightly protruding from his tanned neck. He was a beautiful guy with straight black hair that was wet over his face. His eyes were closed and one of his hands was touching his balls, kind of slightly pinching his sack, while his other hand was rubbing back and forth ever so lightly over his right nipple. I was obviously interrupting a private moment, but who could blame him.

At first he didn't see me, so I thought I could escape undetected. As I tried to make my way past him, the sound of the water moving gave me away and he opened his eyes and in that moment. I froze as I was caught staring at him, and I was nervous. He smiled and asked if it was my first time there and I said "yes." He introduced himself as he walked towards me, making his way through the water and past a couple of large rocks and put out his hand and said, "My name is Trevor."

He was English and his accent was just the thing in that moment to make me all that much more excited the minute he spoke. I took his hand and introduced myself. His strong wet hand in mine felt like, well I can't even tell you what it felt like. I just remember that I couldn't let go of his grip as I stared into his eyes. He understood and with confidence, reached out with his other hand and touched my cock which was starting its journey upward and pointing towards him.

At first I was embarrassed and let go of his hand, but he didn't let go of my ever increasingly erect cock. I gazed around to see if anyone was watching and caught an even bigger surprise. Behind me, above on a large rock were three men in their 20's, a stunning Latin with teal eyes, which glistened in the sunlight. He was standing in the football position, crouched with his hands on his knees and his legs slightly bent and apart on the rock, in full view of the entire garden. One of the other guys was positioned underneath him, buried in the Latin boy's crotch. His face was almost completely hidden within the Latin boy's thighs.

All I could see was his long-brown hair and the side of his face. The third guy was standing next to the Latin boy. His blonde hair and milky complexion were flawless and he kissed the little Latin guy with such passion. I saw all of this in a moment. In the next moment, I was brought back to my own encounter as I felt warmth and that special wetness around my own stiff dick.

The excitement of it all was very intense to say the least. As I moaned, I was drowned out by the falls, but we weren't unnoticed as some other boys were walking towards us and I guess it is a very friendly atmosphere, because before I knew it,

I was in the middle of something overwhelming.

There were at least 6 guys in all and after five more minutes of this, I had to stop and collect myself. As I disentangled myself from the others, I caught a glimpse of Trevor leaning back on a moss covered tree and getting serviced. I knew he wouldn't miss me.

That evening, there was a barbeque and all the hotel guests got a chance to meet one another in a more formal setting, that is, a setting with conversation. But by darkness, the garden was lit by a line of fire from permanent torches and the waterfalls were the most magnificent color of yellow and blue. It was a warm night with a full moon and as I was walking from my room to check out the social scene in the grotto, I bumped into Trevor again on the path and he asked me, "Where did you go before?" and I replied, "The whole group thing is still new to me and it's going to take me some time to get used to it."

He smiled and kissed me lightly and I kissed him back and we kept kissing and the next thing I knew, we were in a small alcove between some bamboo stalks and we made love for what felt like hours. Afterwards we went for a skinny dip and came back to my room. It was really balmy and we fell asleep in my bed.

In the morning, the hotel served a fabulous breakfast complete with fresh fruits, jams, juices and an array of pancakes, waffles, eggs, sausage, bacon, breads...ooh it was wonderful. Of course I started the morning with a Bloody Mary as well. The rest of the weekend was more of the same.

The sex became less important over the course of the weekend against the relaxation and beautiful lushness of it all, the garden, the falls, the food, the sun etc. The sex was however readily available and quite a sight when you saw 15 guys positioned in every which way imaginable in such a setting. All in all I don't think I'll ever forget this past Labor Day.

-S.B. of Hollywood

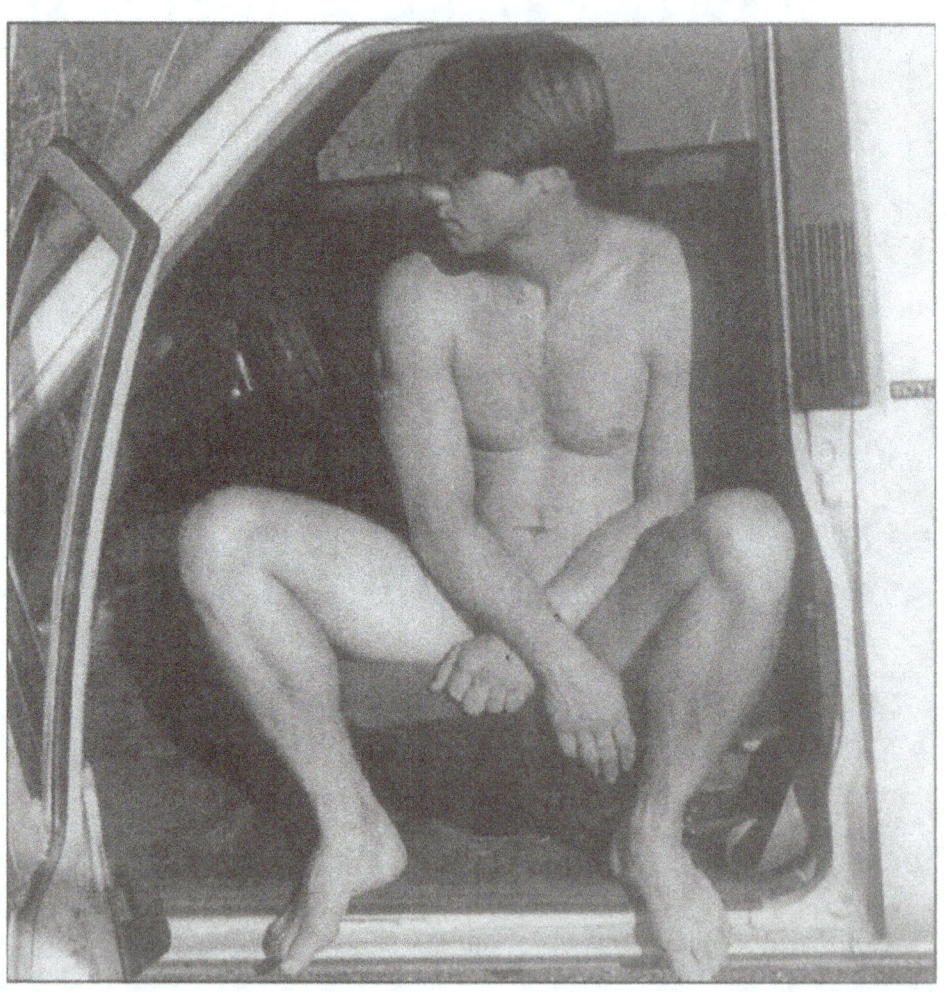

GOOD DRIVE WITH GRANT

DEAR **NAKED MAGAZINE**,

I have a friend who loves to be driven around while nude. His name is Grant, he just turned 22 and he's really, really cute. Here's a story of one of those times.

I picked him up outside his apartment. He was only wearing sandals and some cut-off sweats which were just a bit over-sized. They rode below the normal belt line. It was a very sexy sight. It was just getting dark and because we live in Phoenix, it was a very warm night. As I took off, he removed the sandals and sweats.

I drive a Bronco so we're up higher than other cars. I first headed the cruisy area in Papago Park and drove around but it was kinda slow there so I then drove him to the Superstition Freeway and we headed east. He would alternate from playing with himself to just being another passenger. He's really cute and fun to watch. Luckily for me, he likes to show off.

We drove out past Apache Junction and then north up toward the lakes. It's a very popular drive but we managed to find a quiet place to get out and relax. Of course, it was dark by now but the moon was out (and so was Grant's). He likes to be naked anywhere and was having a good time. He would get hard and then let it go down without cumming. He said it made for a more intense ejaculation later.

We soon started on our way back. I now became a bit more courageous and joined him in nudity. I got hard immediately and after a while became used to it and started to go down. As that would happen, Grant made sure I stayed up. Soon we were passing under downtown and it was bright in that long tunnel. Soon after we passed it Grant said he was ready to shoot, and so was I!

He worked on both of us. I had to make sure I kept the speed limit but it seemed to be driving faster as I got closer. Then, boom! We both came almost at the same time! It was a great release! There was cum dripping all over the interior of my bronco.

I stopped near his apartment to put my stuff back on, and clean up. Grant didn't yet. He waited until I was in front of his apartment to slip on his sweats. He picked up his keys and wallet, said goodnight and bounded into his building. Another fine drive with naked Grant!

- T.J. from Phoenix

CAN NEVER SAY "NO"
TO A NAKED MAN

DEAR **NAKED MAGAZINE**,

A number of years ago, I was driving through the hills of Griffith Park on a sunny weekday afternoon. I passed a pick-up truck with a shell on it, which was parked on one of the turnouts. I glanced over to see if the driver was cute and as I passed I noticed he was standing behind the truck and appeared to be naked. The truck was backed in with its tailgate facing away from the road. I thought I must be mistaken as this is a well-traveled road. I made a U-turn at the next turnout and headed back to check out the situation. As I slowly passed I saw that he was indeed naked. He was a very hot, hairy, older man. I turned around once again at the closest turnout. I came back and parked alongside his truck.

He was no longer standing behind the truck, but he had taken a bicycle out and had leaned it beside the truck. I got out of my car to see if he had walked down into the bushes. When I got to the back of his truck I saw he was laying on his back naked and slowly pumping his huge hard cock. I sat on the tailgate and he nudged me with his foot. I began rubbing his legs until he pulled me inside.

He pulled off my tank top and running shorts and we began feasting on each other's bodies. All the time the tailgate remained open as we brought each other to explosive climaxes. It was one of the hottest experiences that I had ever had. To this day, I can't say "no" to a naked man!

-R.H.B. of L.A.

TRAIL SEX

DEAR **NAKED MAGAZINE**,

It was a beautiful summer day and I decided to go jogging in Griffith Park. I parked my car by the tennis courts and began jogging up the trail that runs alongside and above them. I jogged up and around the dusty trail until I wound my way down to an area above the golf course that can be pretty cruisy. I knew the trail gets pretty steep just ahead, so I decided to look for a place to rest for a bit. There was a foot path just before the main entrance to this area and I turned left and walked a short way up the trail into the bushes. I stopped for a few minutes to rest.

A moment later a stunning young blond came up the trail. I usually don't go for men as young as he was, but he was absolutely breath-taking. He had short blonde hair, cute little blond moustache, swimmer's build with a well-formed chest, and muscular legs. He was only wearing jogging shoes and brief wafer-thin aqua marine colored jogging shorts which perfectly accented his beautiful golden body. As he passed, I breathlessly watched the thin shorts hug his perfectly rounded ass cheeks and ass crack.

He must have been jogging also as the shorts were wet with sweat which dripped down the back of the blonde fur on his muscular thighs. The sweat also made the material semi-translucent and I could see the creamy skin on his magnificent ass. He did not stop, but rounded a corner and disappeared out of sight. I stood there a moment, my heart pounding with passion. I decided I too would walk farther up the hill and hoped that if I was lucky I might get another glimpse at this hot young man.

When I rounded the corner, he stood there naked except for his jogging shoes! Seeing me, he smiled, said "Hi" and leaned back against a rock. The trail was very narrow at this point and I just stood there frozen for a few minutes enjoying the view and not knowing how to react. He began playing with his cock which was already glistening in the sun with pre-cum. I stepped forward and he reached out his arms and embraced me tightly.

Our lips met in a deep passionate kiss. My hands explored the hard muscles of his shoulders and back as we continued our embrace. When they reached his ass cheeks, he moaned softly and started to pull my shirt up and over my head. He began to lick the sweat off my neck, shoulders and upper chest. As he worked his way down to my nipples his hands grasped the waist band of my jogging shorts and pulled them down. His lips and tongue worked their way to my left nipple which he expertly brought to full erection. He then licked his way across my furry chest and gave equal treatment to the other nipple.

I was nervous that someone else would come along, but was too aroused by this magnificent young man with the talented tongue to stop now. He began to bend his knees and as he licked the sweat from my stomach he looked up into my eyes and gave each of my nipples a squeeze with his fingers. I shuddered with passion as he continued looking into my eyes and slowly licked down lower and lower. He licked past my rigid cock and tongued my balls. As he did so, he pushed my shorts all the way to the ground and I stepped out of them and kicked them aside.

This allowed me to spread my legs further apart and he began to lick the sensitive area behind my balls. When I moaned and shuddered again, he stood up, turned me around and began licking the ultra sensitive nape of my neck. He then licked down and over each shoulder, nibbling the shoulder muscles as he worked across and back down the other. He then nibbled my neck again and licked down my spine. He would lick back up to the nape of my neck and then down my spine again each time licking a little lower until he was finally teasing the crack of my ass with his hot tongue.

I spread my legs wide and he slipped his tongue deeply between my cheeks. I'd only been rimmed once before and I gasped loudly as his tongue probed my tender hole. I felt light-headed and had to bend over and grasp the rock to keep from losing my balance. This gave him even better access and his talented tongue probed my ass deeper and deeper. As if this wasn't enough, he began using one hand to stroke my cock as his other hand stroked his own.

He began simultaneously stroking furiously and vigorously lapping my hairy ass crack. Within moments we were both moaning loudly and spraying our hot loads of cum all over the ground! It was so intense, I thought I was going to pass out! I held onto the rock for several minutes waiting for the spasms of pleasure to stop racking my body. When I turned around, he was slipping back into his shorts.

He smiled, winked at me, turned around and jogged off. I cleaned myself up the best I could, got dressed and walked down the trail. As I turned back onto the main trail to head back to my car, I passed a smiling body-builder type who commented, "That was really hot!" I blushed with embarrassment, but smiled ear to ear because of the comment. I never saw that hot young man again, but although this happened almost 15 years ago, I remember it as if it happened yesterday.

- R.H.B. of LA.

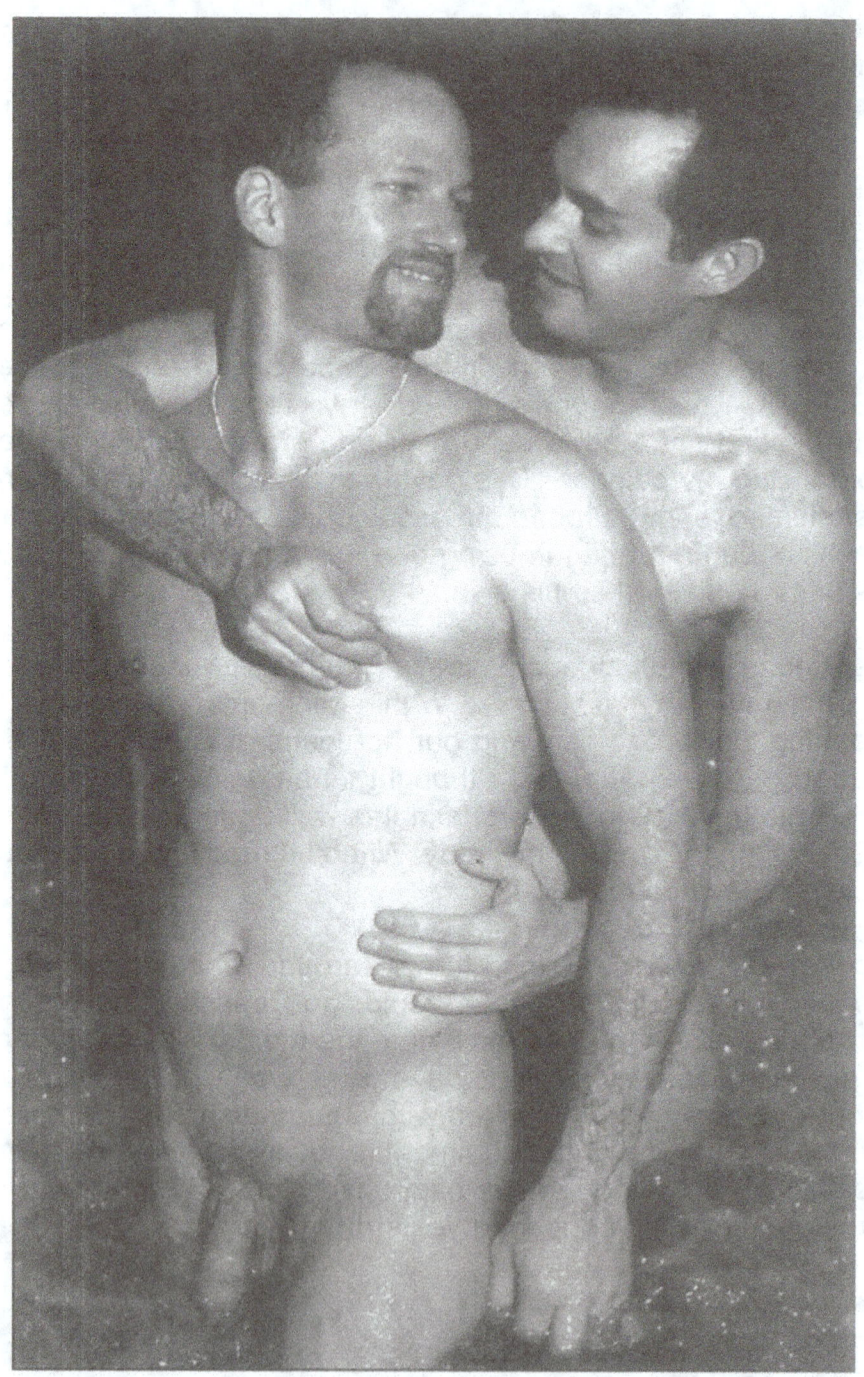

SAME TIME, SAME PLACE

DEAR **NAKED MAGAZINE**,

For those of you that might enjoy trying on your buddy's underwear, here's an interesting situation that happened to me last weekend. I was up in the local mountains sunbathing and dipping into the cool mountain stream in my Speedos. I had the whole place to myself until a nice-looking guy came by and took a spot nearby. We said hello and in a short time he stripped naked and we kept making eye contact. Then I took off my Speedo and went into the stream. He followed me to some warm boulders where we laid and had a wonderful time jacking each other off in this beautiful setting. I shot a pretty big load all over myself and he was about to shoot his when we saw a couple of hikers some distance away, we had just enough time to put something on.

Unfortunately, all my clothes were back at the spot I had been sunning at before, so this guy lent me his Calvin Klein button fly underwear to put on before the hikers got within view. It was hot to put them on and I got instantly hard and was nearly ready to cum again.

After the hikers had past, I took them off and gave them back to him, and apologized for the wet spot on them from the load of cum that was still on me. He didn't mind and maybe enjoyed them being wet. He got up and said he had to go, and that was the end of that. I told him I hoped we would try this again soon! He just smiled and said "same time, same place, next week"! I will write in and tell you what happens!
 - A. of West L.A.

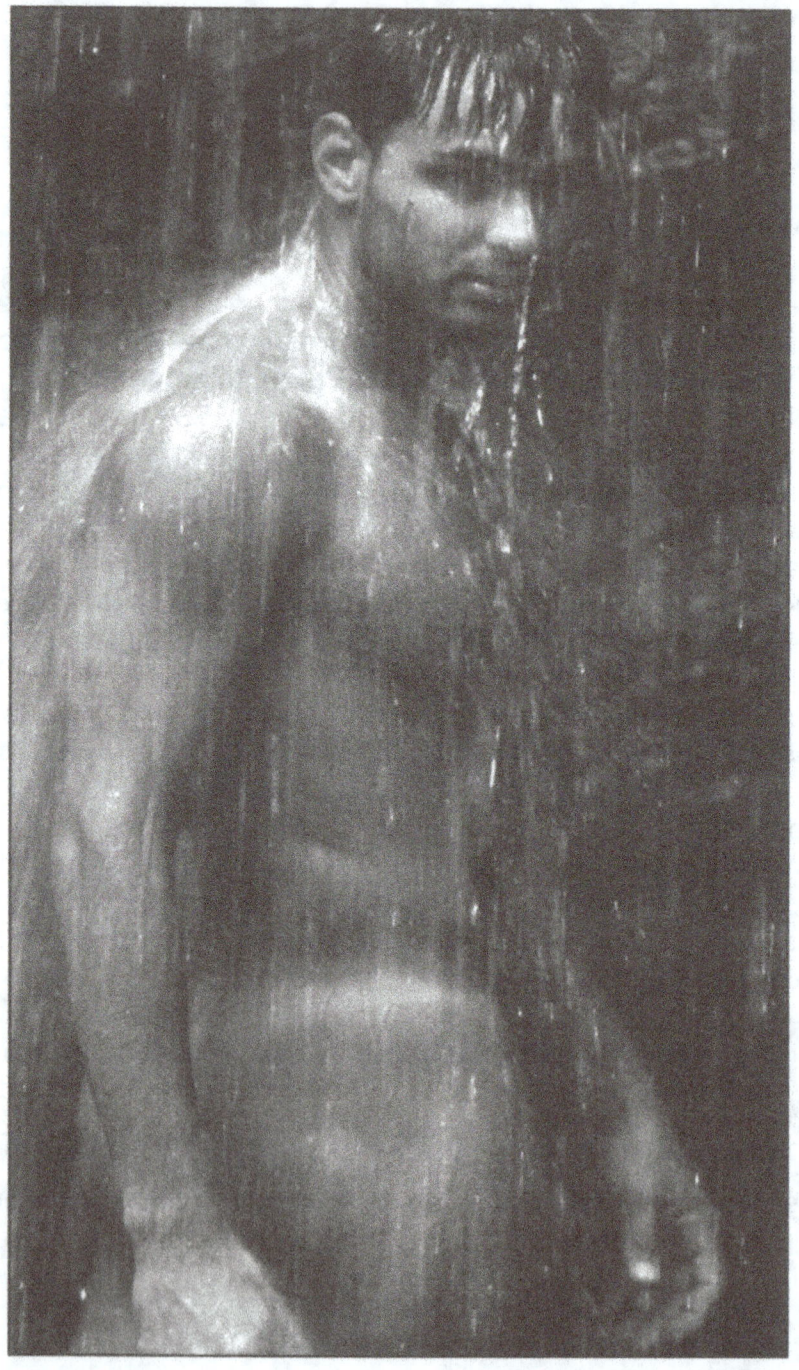

THE VOTE IS STILL OUT

DEAR **NAKED MAGAZINE,**

A true story: I first noticed him at the beginning of my second year of law school at a local, top-ranked school. Steve was his name; he was very cute and obviously had worked out a bit. He wasn't hugely muscular, but he was of nice size and very firm. Of course, once he got to school, the gay network went into full force and tried to find out his story.

He went to the same college as I, but he graduated four years earlier. At least we had something in common to talk about. Well, after about a year of speculation and yearning to touch (or at least see) his fabulous physique, I saw him working out at the student gym. As I had done several times before outside the gym, we started to talk about school, a recent basketball game, etc., and I just felt tantalized again.

After I was finished working out, I went to change in the locker room and decided to take a leak. As I walked in, I saw this totally naked stud, taking a leak, with his back to me flashing one of the nicest, roundest, firmest butts I had ever seen. The stud turned his head towards me and it turned out to be HIM! He nonchalantly said "Hi" and proceeded to finish taking a leak, and then walked over to take a shower. I hadn't planned on doing so, but I quickly undressed and hopped in a nearby shower (close enough to see him soaping up his nuts, dick and ass, but not so close as to be staring).

He didn't get hard or anything, and it was very tough for me not too, I would've done anything at that moment if I could have just walked over there and swallowed every inch of his ripe cock. In the midst of my day dreaming, I didn't even notice that he left the showers! By the time I hurried and washed all the soap off, and got my hard-on to go down. He was already exiting the locker room. The sight of him naked and showering not ten feet away from me, kept me hard and horny and full of fantasies for weeks!

P.S. The vote is still out about him. After all, what do you think about a hot, 32-year-old man who works out and has never been married?

- H. from Los Angeles

HOT SAUNA

DEAR **NAKED MAGAZINE**,

As I write this, I'm only wearing a flannel nightshirt but it's hiked up to my waist, 'cause only my upper body tends to get cold. Lately I've discovered the sauna here at the complex I live in. It isn't used much even though it's great. I've been enjoying going in there and getting naked (alone) and relaxing. I have a towel nearby and in the event someone else comes in. I just cover myself up (unless they're naked, too).

The other night, this one guy did come in...He was first wearing shorts but then he took them off. He looked like he had a really huge unit. The guy was younger than me, probably mid 20's. I have terrible "gaydar" so I couldn't tell whether he was gay or not...at least not at first. He was sitting on the top level and I was sitting on the bottom level (actually, I was laying down with the towel over my groin covering me up)...then he moved down to the same level and sat facing me...that's when I saw his dick and how big it was.

I get easily aroused and I must admit - it took every ounce of willpower I had not to get erect in that sauna when I saw how big his dick was. He wasn't a big muscular guy so on him it seemed really disproportionate to his body and maybe looked bigger than it actually was. There were a couple of moments when my imagination kicked in and I had to cover myself up with my towel.

After being in the sauna for about 30 minutes, I was getting overheated and decided to go to the jacuzzi. He followed...we sat across from each other and soon I felt his foot moving up my leg until it reached my crotch...then he started rubbing my dick with his foot through my shorts (and by now, of course, I was hard).

What's a guy to do in a case like this...I reciprocated ...and, well, to make a long story short, we ended up fondling each other in the jacuzzi. There was one point where he "went under" and gave me head for a bit...but neither of us had an orgasm and when we left the jacuzzi, that was it.

It was just one of those times when a naked guy comes into your life and you really don't know what to do. When it happens again...I'll know how to handle him.

- M. A. from Laguna

UTAH LICENSE PLATE

DEAR **NAKED MAGAZINE**,

An experience for your readers. I drive a Ford Bronco which is also lifted so I sit pretty high. This vantage point gives me some good views into other cars. The other day I was driving up to the mountains to get out of the city for a while. The road is mostly a one-laner. There are always people who want to pass you but can't until we all get to a passing lane.

There was one car that looked like it wanted to pass real bad so when we came to a passing lane I took the right lane as usual (I don't rush when I drive up to the mountains). As it passed, I looked over. I expected it to speed up and pass me but it didn't. It drove up to my side and stayed with me. I looked in and saw a guy driving. He was totally naked. He didn't even have shoes. He looked over and smiled. I liked the way he looked and nodded back at him.

The end of the passing lane was coming up and he drove ahead and then sped away. I thought that was the last I'd see of him but it wasn't. A little later, when I finally almost forgot about it, I noticed his car. I knew it was his because I remember the license plate (it was from Utah). I looked to see if he was in his car but I didn't see him. I went up and turned around to park in a turn-out across the road from his. As I waited to see what was up, I noticed him in the bushes behind the car. He wanted me to see him. He was still naked but this time had sneakers on. He also had a woody and was playing with it.

Cars were still going by infrequently. He would hide when they did. Finally he motioned me to get closer. I started up my bronco and drove over near his car. When there were no cars coming, he came to the passenger side, which I opened up, and he got in. His name was Jack. We talked about the situation and soon he said to drive farther up the mountain with him naked. It sounded good to me, so I continued my drive up the mountain with this good-looking, bare-ass naked passenger with a slick woody next to me. I also got a woody. I was wearing a tank-top and cut-off Levis which were getting uncomfortable as I got harder. I finally stopped briefly to remove them.

We had been driving for a while when he suggested I stop at this specific location. He listened for other cars and when he was satisfied there were none coming, he got out and said to follow him. I put on my shorts and followed him. He went down into a creek and into a rock tunnel that went right under the road we just drove over. There we had a great licking and beat-off session. After which, we drove up farther and then back down to his car. He must have done this many times before with other guys. He knew exactly where to go. We exchanged numbers and have gotten together many times since. It was one of the most erotic experiences of my life.

-V. H. of Burbank

SOUTHERN PLAY

DEAR **NM**,

It was in the south, North Carolina to be exact. My cousin and I (we were only about 18 at the time) were biking through the back farm roads for hours. We raced, pretended we were cops, cowboys and Indians, and Olympic bikers. It was great and we were at it all day long. We had biked so far that there were no houses, barns or anything but acres of crops. Eddie and I had already stripped our shirts off and our shoulders were bright red with the sun.

We stopped to pee along the side of the road, but the only way my cousin could pee was by pulling down his tight shorts all the way because he was wearing a jockstrap. I stood beside him and lifted my shorts to hold my cock and piss too. He pulled his shorts entirely off and stood there in his jockstrap. I swatted his bare butt and we horsed around with our cocks hanging out...they got hard quickly and we were soon jacking.

Ed took his jock strap off and stood there butt-naked jacking. He pulled my shorts down at one point and I stepped out of them. We were really going at it, and then Ed grabbed my shorts and hopped on his bike and took off leaving me there naked. He also left his own shorts and strap on the ground. All I had to do was put them on, but instead I grabbed them and got on my own bike and raced after him.

It was a hell of a sight, two horny boys naked on their bikes. I caught up with him and we pushed each other until we fell off the bikes and were wrestling naked on the side of the road. He ran off into a field and I ran after him. We wrestled and that soon changed into a scene with him on top of me. The feeling of his bare butt sitting on my bare chest was fantastic. I could actually feel his blood pumping in his body. He aimed his cock at my mouth and under the pretense that he had won the fight, I had to suck it.

We sucked until our guts were full of each others loads. He got the backpack from the bikes and returned so we could eat the sandwiches we had purchased and drank some warm soda. We talked and touched each other exploring each others bodies. I lay on my stomach as he laid on top of me and inserted himself into me. We had agreed to try it. I fucked him next...him on his back and me holding his ankles.

We biked, still naked back towards home until it started to get dark and cool. We put each others shorts on without saying a word about it. I wore his jock and tight shorts, he wore my gym shorts and tank top. My Uncle, Ed's father, found us and gave us a ride home in his truck. About a mile away from the house he pulled the truck over and told us to put our own clothes on so there would be no questions at home. I felt myself blush thinking he knew what we had been doing.

We stripped naked in the truck cab. I was embarrassed to be naked in front of my Uncle. Once we were dressed in our own clothing, he continued the drive home. "Want to go biking again tomorrow?" Ed asked once we had finished dinner. I looked at my Uncle and he smiled knowingly and looked at me making me blush. "Sure" I said.

We biked all summer and when I returned home I was ready to fulfill the many fantasies I had been having for a long time with the guys I knew at home. I still jack off thinking about biking naked with Ed along those deserted farm roads.

- R.W. of West Hollywood

PAINTING IS FRUSTRATING

DEAR **NAKED MAGAZINE**,

When I was about 21, a friend got me a job painting a house. It belonged to an older lady and her son. He was about 27 or 28. He lived in a small apartment in the back by the pool. During my time there, I would see him bring over women and go skinny dipping with them. The women usually wore something because of me and/or his mother. I wondered about his mother. This lady was very sweet and seemed foreign.

I wondered if she ever looked out at him/them? He didn't seem to care if she did or not, he swam naked a lot. Anyway I had a good time pretending not to notice. He had a fine, slim, above-average body. It soon became irritating because I couldn't do anything about it. I would have loved to have joined him but, of course, I finally finished painting the house and never went back. It was just one of those stories that I thought your reader's might be interested in. Did anyone have any similar experiences?

- R.O. of Van Nuys

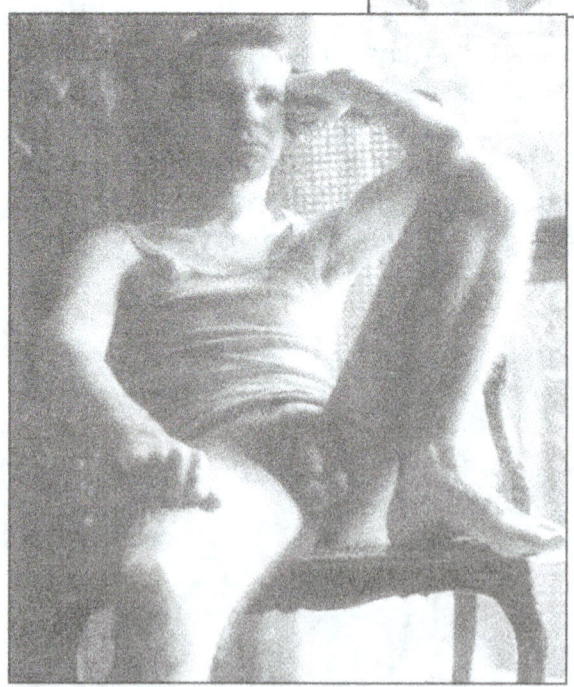

NUDE SIGHTING

DEAR **NAKED**,

A short nude-sighting story: My friend and I decided to go to the Long Beach Gay Pride Festival one year. I went over to his house in West Hollywood early the Sunday morning of the event. As I was waiting for him to finish getting ready, I stood near his second-story window looking down to the street.

I soon noticed a long haired man sipping a cup (of coffee, I presume) in the window across the street. He was as naked as a babybird, standing at the window and looking out to the street, as well! He was on the first floor, so I could see more than any-one on street level. He looked around and finally saw me.

He stepped away from the window and that's the last I saw of him. I told my friend about it. He didn't believe me, saying he never had that kind of luck. It wasn't a big deal but it's fun to mention. At least I enjoyed it!

- A.E. from Studio City

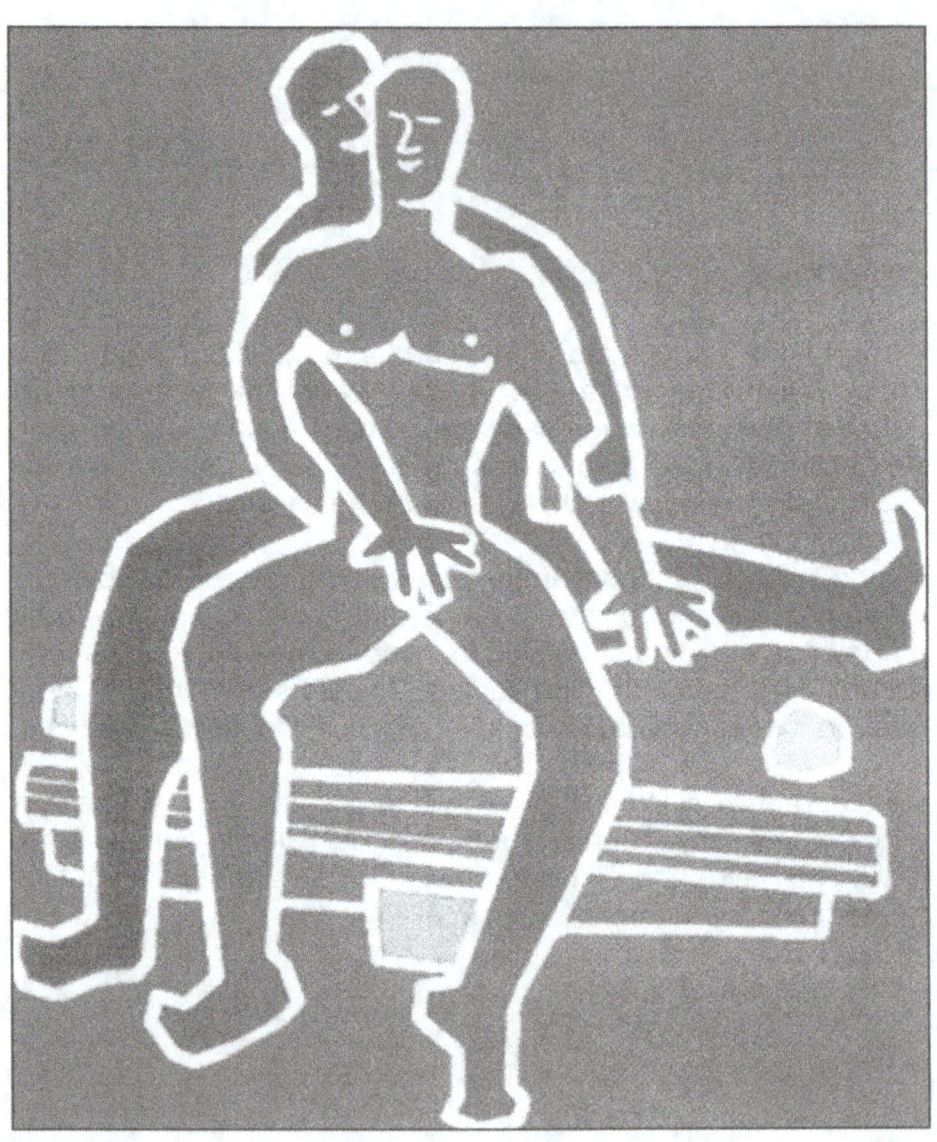

WINDOW WATCHING

DEAR **NAKED MAGAZINE**,

A few years ago, I visited Palm Springs and stayed in one of the clothing-optional resorts. Of course, I and a few others went naked everywhere but most guys wore a swimsuit or more. There was this one couple that was really attractive. Both were naked all the time and smooching whenever they could.

The evening of my first day, I got dressed to go out to eat. On my way out, I passed a window of the room where this couple was staying. They were sitting on the couch naked watching TV. I just passed by because I didn't want to be known as a gawker. This window by the way was facing the street and could be seen from the street with a little bit of elevation. Anyway, on my way back in, I again passed the window. I had to stop because of what I saw this time.

They were engaged in a hot and heavy session of man-to-man sex right there on the couch. Of course, now I understood. They wanted to be watched. So I did. I stayed and watched them for a while. They noticed me and smiled, then went right back into it. I would catch one or the other glimpsing toward the window to see if I (or anyone else, for that matter) was still there.

They did everything. It was a live porn video with interactive action, sort of. They finally both came and slumped down onto the couch embracing, kissing, and smiling at each other. I left for my room where I proceeded to fantasize about what I had just seen. I hit the wall behind my head with my cum. Something I haven't done in a while. I wonder if these guys make it a habit to allow others to watch? I hope so, other guys should experience what I did!

- G.D. from Denver

PATIO PLEASURES

DEAR **NAKED MAGAZINE**,

One evening, actually about one in the morning, standing on the balcony watching a gentle rain and thinking it would probably stop most of the skinny dippers, I caught motion out of the corner of my eye. A man had come into his apartment on the first floor of the building perpendicular to mine, and my eye caught the living room light going on.

His patio door drapes were mostly closed, but where they didn't quite meet at the center I could see him as he moved to the kitchen, return quickly with what I assume to be a beer in his hand and go to other parts of the apartment. His next pass was more interesting because he'd stripped down to his underwear. The kitchen light went off and I again saw him pass the drape opening, in his underwear. A moment later the living room light went out and I thought he was on his way to bed.

My glance went back to the pool area and I was about ready to go in to bed myself when I heard a sound. I looked toward his apartment as the patio door opened and saw him pull back the drapes and peer out. He was holding the drape in his left hand to cover himself from the waist down. He looked about for a moment then the drape fell from his hand as he went back inside, but he didn't close the door. I found myself excited. Perhaps this guy would open the drapes or step out in his briefs. Even that would be nice!

I watched as his right arm extended outside, pushing the drape aside. His inside lights were out, but the security light above his balcony lit him well enough to see a nicely tanned body, accented in the white underwear, standing there; a beer in the right hand and a cigarette in the left. The light rain continued but didn't block the view.

He stood there, smoking his cigarette, finally flipping it out onto the wet grass. He stepped onto the small cement patio area, still somewhat protected from detection by the walls at either end of the patio. He moved to either wall, peering around it to see who might be about. Looking towards me he would be staring directly into the security light and unable to see me. Satisfied that he was alone and unobserved and with his left hand free, he reached into his underwear to 'arrange' himself!

He massaged it for several seconds before slipping his hand out and started sniffing his fingers! I guess he was feeling sure of his situation because he moved to the very edge of his pad, which made him a bit more vulnerable to view. The left hand went behind him, I guess to scratch his butt, then came around front again, inside his shorts, to his cock. He groped himself and I could plainly see the stroking motion going on inside his underwear. He took a drink from his beer and he hand-crushed the can. As he turned towards his open door, the bulge in his briefs told me of his erection, and it was a nice lump indeed! He disappeared inside, but again the door did not close. By now, I was raving hard and beginning to drip!

A short time later, the curtains again moved and he stepped out to the porch, a fresh beer in his left hand. He again moved to each end of the porch and peered around his walls to check out the scene, the lump in his shorts still very present. Again, satisfied that he was unobserved, he took a step off his porch barefoot onto the grass, looking around. He took another step, and another, moving towards a tree that stood between him and the fence around the pool.

Car headlights from the entrance to the complex caused him to rush back to his porch. He stood there for a moment as the headlights disappeared, then again moved towards the tree. He made it all the way this time, and stood with his back against the tree, his left foot on its trunk propping him on the right foot. He was facing me, but somewhat covered by the tree.

Fortunately, the limbs did not block my view of his midsection. He again slipped the right hand into his shorts. The motion was even more pronounced than before. His hand slipped from the short's waistband and re-entered at the opening for his right leg. He pulled his cock out the leg opening, moved his hand into position and slipped the shorts aside so his balls hung freely, too! As far as I could tell from my distance and the dim light, it was a nice-sized cock, his hand barely fitting around it, and its length looking as if two hands would work better to manipulate it.

He stroked gently for a short time, sipping his beer and no doubt getting off on the fact that he was doing this outside where anyone might be able to see him. My own load was near spewing when he moved back towards the porch. From the back, his tight underwear displayed a firm, rounded ass that looked very edible.

His cock and balls were still hanging out of those shorts as he moved. On the porch, he reached into his briefs with that right hand to scratch his ass, the briefs dropping slightly exposing the sultry top of his crack, (where my tongue desperately wanted to be). He turned around, and the cock was standing very straight out in front of him, casting a long shadow down his left leg. He tilted the beer can high and emptied it, crushing it in his hand, then stepped into his apartment. He apparently only wanted to drop off the can, because he reappeared almost instantly, but without a beer or cigarette...both hands were free.

The rain had nearly stopped, only a fine mist fell now. The guy stood there on his porch, legs spread wide, stroking himself with his left hand while his right was out of sight behind him. He would stroke slowly, sometimes stopping to cup his balls, then stroke vigorously for a moment. He finally got tired of the restriction of the underwear. His legs came together, one hand on each side at the waistband, and they went to his ankles. He stepped out with the left foot, and then flipped the shorts to his hand with the toes of his right foot.

His pubic area was very large and very dark in the dim light, making the size of his standing meat even more impressive. He turned to the door, pulling the drapes aside and throwing the briefs into the apartment. His ass was all I thought it would be...very firm and ready to be eaten! His right hand came to his ass and it was obvious he was scratching his asshole, not the cheek! If a finger was going in, I couldn't tell from my vantage point. I was so close to shooting my balls ached terribly.

He strolled, now stark naked, back out to the tree. He again took the same pose. His right hand remained behind him as he stroked with a regular rhythm on his still stiff dong. He soon increased tempo until I heard what I thought was a muffled groan. The stroking slowed quickly, and then his hand released the stiff meat and shook as if to flail away something sticky! He moved slowly back to the porch, turned one final time to do a slow stroke down the now deflating prick and shake the head off. He disappeared into the apartment as I spewed my own load out into the night.

- Naked Carl

TRIP TO THE HARDWARE

DEAR **NAKED MAGAZINE**,

May 25. 1990 - I pulled into Builder's Square parking lot near work. I noticed a lone white pickup truck parked at the far end of the lot, all by itself, with only one person in it. I drove up that way, by the lawn and garden shop, as if looking for an entrance, and verified he was alone. I figured he was another parking lot jerk-off, as I've seen so often. When leaving the store, I saw a car parked by the truck. Now there were two silhouettes and definitely saw the one on the passenger side lean over towards the driver's side.

I drove out by the back road. As I passed, the passenger was again coming up from the seat. The exit I used leads to another parking area up a slight hill. I stopped there for a few minutes, looking down at the truck. The movements gave the situation away. The driver's right arm moved to the passenger's butt, then around front. The passenger's head was obviously in the driver's lap. The driver now had his right hand on the back of his passenger's head. I had hoped the driver might open his door to step out for some reason.

I finally had to leave to keep from becoming too suspicious myself. As I started to pull away, the passenger sat upright. The driver appeared to be shifting as if to pull up his pants, without a lot of success. Then what I was hoping for all along: the driver's door opened and stepped out. My view was perfect. The driver stood there, his pants down around his knees, his bare butt glowing in the bright sunlight. He was quite a nice-looking guy, probably in his thirties, and in very good shape.

I could see his ass cheeks tighten a couple of times. He leaned over slightly to grip the pants, and turned my direction as he pulled them up. His still very erect prick stuck very straight out in front of him, and even from my distance, I could tell he was well-endowed, probably seven to eight inches at least.

He pulled the khaki pants to his waist, the stiff cock protruding through the opening. He leaned back against the side of his truck for a moment, as if to catch his breath, his right hand stroking his meat several times. He seemed oblivious to the fact that a car was passing his location as this happened, and it's driver slowing to a near stop to watch the activity. As he grasped himself and forced the stiff rod back into his pants, barely able to zip up over it, the car moved on towards the exit.

As the man got back into the truck and the door closed, his passenger got out and moved off to the car parked close by. My view of him was not so good with the truck in the way. To say the least, it was a grand trip to the hardware store!

- Naked Carl

DOOR TO DOOR SALESMAN

DEAR **NAKED MAGAZINE**,

Aug 10. 1990 - The doorbell rang just as I finished my sandwich. It was 6 p.m. I checked the peephole and in the still very bright daylight saw a young man standing there...no doubt selling something. He looked to be a fresh graduate. He had dark hair and nice face, but not pretty. His body wasn't fat, but no athlete either. He was dressed very typical: jeans, t-shirt and tennis shoes. I was stark naked...as usual.

I opened the door and spoke to him through the storm door. Its screen panel at the top permitted us to talk, while the solid bottom section obscured his view of me below the waist. He must have been curious about my lack of shirt and edged closer to the door where he could now see in and note that I was indeed naked. He started his pitch, selling subscriptions to a local newspaper or something.

I asked if he minded if I was nude. He said no. I opened the door and he came in. He followed me to the kitchen. I got out my checkbook, and wrote out a check. His downward gaze as he wrote my receipt was far too long. He was staring at my bare and growing prick. When he could no longer maintain this posture without questions, he passed on the receipt and moved towards the front door.

I followed him, saying thanks for stopping by. He turned to tell me he hoped I enjoyed the paper, but his eyes never met mine! He was too intent on staring at my now erect cock. He stepped through the door, pausing on the porch as if to carefully let the door close without a sound. But I stopped it before it completely closed and pushed it open again. He stepped into the yard, turning to watch as I stroked myself. This was a total turn-on that brought about a fast nice orgasm a few seconds later.

He had moved on a few steps, but stood in my yard watching as I shot my wad onto the porch. I could see the bulge growing in his pants. He groped his bulge to adjust himself then turned and walked to the next house. I doubt he had another subscriber provide quite such a show in this neighborhood!

- Naked Carl

POOL BOY

DEAR **NAKED MAGAZINE**,

(Date not recorded - late at night) I stepped onto the balcony of my third floor apartment, with it's excellent view of one of the five pools in the apartment complex. There had recently been one of those quickie summer thunderstorms, leaving the delightful fresh fragrance in the night air, but with the usual heavy humidity for which Atlanta is known. I heard splashing in the pool. I carefully stepped forward and looked out.

Three guys were in the pool playing around. I couldn't yet see if they were naked. From the sounds of things, they had been drinking and their words frequently spoke of straight sexual matters. They splashed each other and carried on for another few minutes, and then one of them came out of the pool. Unfortunately, he was wearing either a bathing suit or colorful briefs. The others soon followed, also clothed. Oh well, can't always have it your way!

They left the pool and walked off towards another part of the complex. I could hear their voices for another couple of minutes after they were out of sight. The water in the pool had nearly settled to a calm surface when I noticed movement at the fence near the far end of the enclosed pool area. Someone was walking by and had now stopped. He looked towards the pool. I could see he was just wearing shorts. He quickly came over the fence into the pool area.

He walked the full skirt, looking around and then returning to the spot where he started. Apparently satisfied that no one was about, he quickly slipped off the shorts and stepped into the deep end of the pool. The movement was far too fast for me to get any crotch detail, other than spotting the dark patch of pubic hair. He bobbed to the surface and swam the length of the pool.

He stopped just below me, in the shallows and stood for a moment squeezing the water out of his hair. The water line was just below his navel and I could still make out only a dark spot of hair. He dropped into the water again, swimming the pool and stopping at the spot where his shorts lay waiting. In the deep end, he rested with his arms on the skirt, the water now halfway up his torso. He stopped only a moment then again returned to the shallow end.

This end was near me and provided a much better view of the man. He was in his twenties and had very dark, perhaps black hair that sparkled in its wetness. The man stood there, pulling his hair back away from his face. His body was turning slowly as he did this until he was directly facing the security light below my balcony...the only source of light on the pool area at night. His upper torso was beautiful. He obviously had a great tan and his body had that nicely firm look that only comes from working out regularly. Not much body hair visible.

This was a beautiful sight and my cock hardened to the point where it was sticking straight out. I was naked myself as was my habit at home and certainly out here on my dark balcony. I waited...hardly daring to breathe lest he hear me and run! He continued stroking his wet hair and turning slowly in the water. This end of the pool had steps out to the skirt. I watched as he moved slowly to those steps and began his ascension! He glanced quickly in all directions as he came up each step. Two steps and the water level was below his crotch. Now I could see not only the dark patch of pubic hair but the light reflecting off his wet cock. It hung flaccid, probably just over four inches of meat moving as he took his steps. A few more steps and he stood there, stark naked and dripping on the pool skirt. He stood there for a moment, shaking off the water, then stroking his cock and balls.

He walked very slowly around the skirt of the pool, stopping occasionally to look around, until he reached his shorts. His ass was beautiful! Perfect globes of very firm flesh, slightly lighter in tone than the rest of his tanned body. His cheeks moved to accent his walking. He stopped at his shorts. I was afraid he was going to put them on. Instead, he sat on the pool skirt with his feet in the water. He again looked all around then spread his legs slightly. His right hand moved between his legs and the motion was obvious...he was stroking his meat. From this distance, I couldn't see the cock in his hand but I knew what he was doing. He leaned back on the left hand, his torso at a 45-degree angle, his hand now stroking faster. He moved the left hand and lay back. Now I had a much better view of this nice-looking man laying naked by the pool, jerking off!

I nearly came myself. At this moment, I heard a sound, as of voices in the distance and so did the man by the pool. He bolted upright as two figures came into view walking along the sidewalk outside the pool fence. He slid as quietly as possible into the water. The two figures continued walking, either not noticing him at all or not caring that someone was in the pool at this hour. I doubt they could have seen that he was naked as quickly as he'd gotten out of sight in the water.

The two passed in just seconds. Apparently his moment had been spoiled and he needed to get the juices flowing again. He swam the twenty or so feet to the pool ladder and climbed out. Again, a nice ass! He pulled his hair back and started walking slowly towards me. When he reached my end of the pool, he was standing sideways giving me a view of his erection which was standing at about a 45-degree angle, pointing towards the sky.

He stroked himself with his right hand, the left behind him massaging or probing. His hands dropped to his sides. He walked, looking about constantly, toward the fence just below me. A moment later he was leaning quite comfortably along the fence as if all was normal.

He moved back towards the pool then veered back along the fence at several spots. He made his way back towards his shorts. He picked them up but didn't put them on. He casually walked towards the entrance of the pool area, passing the restroom and showers, then down the corridor where he was out of my view.

In a moment, he reappeared outside the pool enclosure and strolled along the sidewalk below my balcony, his right hand stroking his overly-hard cock, his left hand holding onto his shorts. He turned at the end of the fenced area, walking away from me now. At the other edge of the pool enclosure, he again turned to his right, strolling along the sidewalk until he was totally out of my sight.

I assume and hope, that he returned to his apartment this way...stark naked, cock hard, hand stroking that beauty, with his only article of clothing in his left hand. I shot my load and watched it fly over the balcony rail and fall three flights down onto the sidewalk below.

- Naked Carl

JOCKSTRAP

DEAR **NAKED MAGAZINE**,

I just want to say how much I enjoy the fact that this magazine exists. In this careful age of safe sex and teetering gay rights issues, it's nice to have something as pure and daring as a magazine devoted simply to nakedness. Being naked is universal. It's not specifically gay. It's not unsafe (sexually). Yet, it is deliciously forbidden and can be a great turn on.

I am not a 'nudist' per se, yet I'd like to share this experience with everyone. My lover and I were invited to go camping at Joshua Tree on Easter with his cousin and her fiancé. I thought, "Great, stuck in the middle of the desert with a couple of straight people, how exciting." The first day, they decided we should all go rock climbing. Something we've never done. I looked up at these amazing monoliths of stone at the climbers scaling them; little barely clad bodies clinging and crawling up ridiculous slopes. I was a little nervous. Of course, they chose the largest formation they could find. They went around to the other side and said they'd meet us at the top.

My first reaction was to hike back to the car, turn on the radio and the a/c, and relax until they got back. But we decided it was worth a try. A wonderful thing began to happen. We approached this wall of rock and simply said, "Let's do this," and began to climb. Now, I've been climbing trees all my life. At parties in college, I'd wedge between the narrow walls of a hallway and climb to the ceiling. But this! This was amazing. There was nothing like it. If you haven't tried it yet, do yourself a favor and go! There's nothing like hanging a good 35' drop onto rocks and trusting yourself to slowly pull one foot, leg, and hand at a time slowly up the side of these boulders.

It took us just under an hour to reach the flat top. It appeared we were there first. We both felt so charged, so energized. It's an incredible feeling of accomplishment to "conquer" this hugely intimidating structure. Looking out across the desert scale is completely breathtaking. There are no cars, buildings, or telephone poles to gauge anything by. The rock formations are mammoth. The flat floor stretches out eternally. The sky never ends.

We were completely soaked in sweat. I wanted to make full use of the dry wind up there, so I took my shirt off. My lover looked over the other side and saw that our straight couple would be at least another twenty minutes. He took his shirt off. Smiling playfully, I took off my shorts so I was just in my jock. He followed silently playing along.

Then simultaneously, we whipped off the rest of our clothes (shoes and socks included) and started running around on the small platform of the rock. We must have been at least 175' up from the floor. It seemed like a thousand though. We were hooting like some idiot tribe of pale Indians, completely high off the sensations of accomplishment and freedom. Our sweaty clothes were bunched next to the edge. We were playing a dangerous game of grab-ass at each other.

I was balancing next to our clothes and panicked as my lover came at me, swinging myself back around from the edge. As I did, I neatly kicked the clothes off the cliff. Luckily enough, my shorts landed about 10' down. My shirt was hanging dangerously off a precipice. My lover's shorts were just above that. His shirt and both our socks and shoes remained in a safe pile.

He smiled and walked over to me, "Guess who's gonna have to get those, Geronimo!" So, naked, I scaled slowly down the rock face to retrieve our clothes. It was truly a bizarre game of beat the clock. His cousin and her fiancé (did I mention he was a homophobe from Alabama?) were quickly rounding up the other side. He dressed in what remained, while I carefully lowered myself to at last grab my shorts. I couldn't find my jock anywhere and I wasn't about to risk my life for a tee-shirt.

I truly felt closer to nature than ever, my naked body scraping rock as I hung dangerously. I cannot begin to explain the mixture of excitement, fear, freedom, and absolute hilarity of the situation. We were laughing and gasping as I carefully hooked my shorts on my foot and brought them up to my hand. With that secured, I quickly grabbed my lover's shorts and tossed them up to him. It was a bad throw and he missed. "Jesus Christ!" he half-laughed, half-yelled.

He was wearing his shoes and tee-shirt only. "Here, take mine," I said as I tossed them up and went after his. He caught mine and I went after his. Grabbing them and practically hanging from one hand, I pulled them on just as our companions' heads peeked over the other side.

"They're already here," I heard his cousin say. Then, seeing me panicking up the side to get to my shoes and socks she told him, "Oh, honey, look at that!" indicating the view opposite. He finally turned back around and I greeted them shirtless, while tying my shoes. My lover was completely dressed, but my shorts were definitely a size too small. Her fiancé looked at us with suspicion. "What happened to your shirt?" he asked. Barely able to contain myself I replied, "Oh, the wind grabbed it. It's down there and I didn't feel like going after it." With that, he seemed satisfied.

They decided we should all go down the same side (the side my lover and I had climbed up). We passed my shirt on the way down. My lover's shorts were a little big for me and I wasn't wearing any jock strap, so I had to be careful not to be above anyone. When we finally reached the bottom, exhausted and exhilarated, I heard her fiancé exclaim, "Oh, man, GROSS." We walked over to him cautiously. He was bent over looking at something. "What is it, honey?" she said "Somebody left their jockstrap here." She turned and looked at our reddened faces. We looked at each other and all three of us burst out laughing. He just looked on dumbfounded.

- Joshua

ISLAND OF LOVE

DEAR **NAKED MAGAZINE**,

It's great to see other's enjoying nudity as much as my lover and I do! I'd like to tell you all of a special nude escapade we had just this last summer. We decided to visit my grandparents in Upstate New York. They live by a lake. While we're there, we'd have full use of the boat. I'd been all over the lake in previous years and knew all of the secluded and remote places I could show Mike. There's one in particular that I think we could have a little fun on!

The day after arriving at my grandparent's house, we put on our swimming suits and took the boat out on the lake. It was unusually warm weather in that area of the country last summer, so it was great for boating. With a grin on my face, I headed towards the island in the middle of the lake. It was a fun island with lots of trees, rocks and open areas. When Mike saw where I was headed, he kinda knew what I was up too. After he tied the boat to a tree, we grabbed our stuff and began the hike up the rocks to the top of the small island.

Being a bit larger island than it looks, it was quite a hike and we were really hot now! I showed Mike where to store the stuff and then I showed him where we could dive off the rocks into the lake. Since nobody was around, we shucked our swimming suits and played cliff-divers in the buff, diving into the cool water 30 feet below. Well, after climbing back up to the diving point about 10 times, we were both bushed. After getting back to our secluded spot, I spread out a blanket and we took a nap, naked in the sun on an island with camps and people just a half mile away! Where we were, they couldn't even see us with binoculars, so we were safe. It was quite a rush knowing what we were doing, though!

I was sleeping when I felt the familiar feel of Mike's mouth down below. Within minutes, we were both attacking each other like animals in heat and the sex was incredible, to say the least! It was great to be naked in the sun with the one you love, having great sex, and with other people so close! I suppose it's the exhibitionist in all of us but we were extra turned on by this and it made it that much better! As dusk came, we had to head back.

We remained naked as we hiked down to the boat and enjoyed the still-warm air all over our bodies while skimming across the waves, in the semi-darkness, back to the house, and finally slipping on our swim suits as we came into the dock. It was great and we hope to do it all over again, and more, next summer!

-naked Jeff

NOT MY FAULT

DEAR **NAKED MAGAZINE**,

Here's a short true story that happened to me very recently. I had just gotten out of the shower at the gym and was standing at my locker located near the emergency-exit door. While I was standing there, completely naked, an old, Asian man was leaving. He must have been a bit confused because he tried to leave through that emergency-exit door. I thought the alarm would go off, but it didn't. So he opened the door and looks out. It opens onto a very well-used walkway that goes back to the parking lot.

The old guy just stands there with the door wide open, not going out, while men and women are passing by and looking in at me and the other guys in the locker area. I wanted to yell at him to close the door but held back. I didn't say anything because I felt I might 'look' uncomfortable. Finally a guy yells at him to either go out or close the door. He closed the door but did not go out. He finally finds his way out the correct exit.

While the door was open, I was embarrassed about being naked and vulnerable but at the same time, a little excited about being seen naked by anyone who happened to pass by. Actually, only one woman and two guys walked by during this time. I surprised myself by not covering up. I felt that it wasn't my fault and that I was supposed to be naked there in the locker room. If someone looked in, well, so what!

The woman looked in and quickly looked away but the two guys, passing separately, looked in and kept looking as they passed. They also smiled, which I liked. Well there's my true story!

-Naked (but not my fault) Rusty

PARTY

Dear **NM**,

Enclosed is a submission for your Reader's Experiences section. This isn't a sexual story. But it was a unique experience for me and the friend who went along.

Last fall, a friend of mine named George and I decided to go see a play which had been running in Chicago for nearly two years. Everyone we knew who had seen it said it was exceptional, so we figured it was high time we saw it as well. That particular week the gay papers were running an ad for PARTY (the play's name) with a little box below it featuring a special performance: "Naked Night at PARTY" George and I saw the ad and said, almost at the same time, "that's the performance we have to see." We immediately phoned for and got reservations.

The next day we received a call telling us the show was off do to a potential conflict with the City of Chicago's public nudity ordinance.

After several days of going back and forth, the theater sold the house to a Gay Naturist group which, in turn, sold tickets to their members, as well as the general public.

On the appointed night, George and I drove into the city for the play. I had a friend's phone number written on my hand, a precaution he insisted upon in case the place was raided. It hadn't really settled in on us, until we were on the road, what we were about to do. This was a first for both of us; we've never been naked in public before, save the locker room. Both of us gave passing thought to the question of whether or not we'd be comfortable or embarrassed.

When we arrived at the theatre, we were given plastic grocery bags and shown to our seats. Following the example of the others in the room, we stripped off, put our clothes in the bags and sat down to await the beginning of the show. Of course, we also discreetly checked out everyone else in the place. That in itself was interesting since, in this context, no one cared.

A little unexpectedly, we felt no self-consciousness or discomfort. We talked to those close to us as easily as we would have in any crowd, if not more easily. It didn't matter that we were all nude, we were just comfortable.

Everyone in the play's cast ended up naked on stage by the end of the show. It's a twist of comic irony that when the performance started the actors on stage had more clothing on that the audience.

-Greg from Chicago, IL

THE DARE OF ALL DARES

Dear **Naked Magazine**,

A friend told me of your magazine and I am glad that there's finally a publication dealing with the issues of nudity. I'm not a nudist, but am very much into being nude in public and seeing others nude in public.

I'll share one of my experiences with you. I enjoy taking off my clothes in public whenever possible, and seeing other guys do the same, especially nude streetwalking. It's thrilling, invigorating and sexually very exciting for me like nothing else.

One afternoon, about 2 p.m. on a weekday, I did a scene on a NYC subway platform. I was with a friend (also into public nudity) who dared me to get naked and pump my butt-hole with my finger. There were only five people at the other end of the platform. I took off every piece of clothing and left them on the ground, shoes and socks as well.

I began walking, completely nude and hard, up the platform toward the people. I could feel the cold wind of the tunnel blowing up my ass and around my hard dick. The cold, platform felt exciting under my bare feet. I got just behind a staircase where the people were, and laid down on the platform. I spread my legs in the air and began finger-fucking my ass.

As I was about to cum, I got up and walked over to the people and said, "hey everybody, look at me!" My friend came running with my clothes as fast as he could. I shot a stream of cum across the platform, as we both ran out of the station as fast as we could, a shame, because it felt so good! It was weird how natural it felt to be in the subway nude.

-David from New York, NY

CLUELESS CROTCH

Dear **Naked Magazine**,

An English pen-pal was visiting the USA for the first time and the two of us boarded a very crowded bus to go see the Phoenix Zoo (in AZ). It was hotter than the pits of hell outside, and the bus was full to capacity. We had no choice but to thread our way to the back of the bus and hope for the best.

However, when we got back there, we found two empty spaces directly behind an extremely hunky teenager about eighteen or nineteen who was passed out across one entire side, the back area behind him was strangely vacant...I assumed it was due perhaps to the over powering ripeness... which presented no problem to my friend and me...so we calmly sat down.

I immediately discovered the reason why no one else had taken the seats, as the view down the wide tunnels of the guys' baggy cotton shorts was sheer heaven! He not only had on ZERO underwear, but also his hairy legs descended into a jungle of curly black crotch hair which nested therein, about a pound of prime, uncut prick!

However, to get a really good view, one would have to lean slightly...and peer obviously, as his legs were spread wide. I struggled with the weighty dilemma for a few moments. I then glanced up to see if anyone else was taking this in. I saw (to my delight) a very broad grin upon the face of another male passenger who was seated facing the side seat.   He had undoubtedly read my mind.

Thus encouraged, I leaned forward and took in the sights. The smiling guy laughed out loud. My friend then also bit the bullet and took a peek. We rode thus for perhaps fifteen more minutes before the bus driver slammed on this brakes and the passenger-of-delight awoke, at which he rather grumpily sat up (without a clue) and got up and got off the bus. Later, at home, I got off too!

-Bud from Phoenix, AZ

HITCHHIKER HOOKUP

Dear **NAKED**,

It took place on a Saturday in the middle of May in 1993. I left my apartment around 6 a.m. to drive out to the western part of the state to pick someone up. I had just pulled onto the highway near my home when I saw a young man hitching a ride, He was blond, I'd say early 20's, and wearing a t-shirt and shorts. Since I was in no particular hurry, I decided to stop and pick him up.

He had an overnight bag which he tossed into the back seat before climbing into the passenger seat. After introductions, he told me he was staying with relatives at their summer home about 60 miles away. He asked me a few questions, ending with some reference to my wife. I laughed and said there was no wife.

By now, we'd been driving nearly ten minutes. I then noticed the tip of his penis sticking out of the right leg of his shorts. He played with it a bit and my looks apparently reassured him. He soon had it pulled out the top of his shorts rubbing it.

By the twenty-mile mark, the shorts were down around his ankles. Mind you, I wasn't saying anything, just driving and watching.

By thirty miles everything, including shoes, was off and he sat naked beside me stroking his more than ample cock. He asked me to keep my hand on his inside left thigh, which I did without hesitation. Heading down the highway at sixty mph, it was tough to watch as much as I would have liked. I would let him know when a truck was coming up behind us and he would cover up for a moment.

He told me he loved being naked, especially in front of someone. As we neared his relative's home, he had not yet climaxed, so he told me to drive on a bit. He had me pull into a deserted parking lot while he finished his duty by impressing me with his hot cum shot. He pulled his clothes back on, and I then drove him back and dropped him off at the house... unfortunately never to see or hear from him again.

-Kent from Provincetown

EXHAUSTING BIKE RIDE

Dear **NM**,

A quick naked story.   In west LA, few activities can beat mountain biking in the Santa Monica Mountains. Clean air (most of the year), incredible plant life, flowing water in the creeks and either total isolation or from time to time, other mountain bikers.

One of them passed me on a long fire road.   He had rippling legs, a long lean body and was in excellent shape. He glanced back, then he was gone.

About a half an hour later, I came down a steep trail into a canyon and suddenly saw his bike lying on some rocks. SHIT! I thought he had crashed...or was he cruising?

I stopped my bike. No sign of him. Then, he came around the rock. "Hey," he said. "Hey, is everything alright" I replied. He chuckled and said "yes". We talked about bikes for a minute and I could feel myself getting hard. I could see he was too. He suggested I follow him. We rode down the trail and then off a smaller path.

He took off his shirt and dropped his bike. His back muscles and stomach were toned, smooth, nearly flawless. His chest was solid without bulging. He had long hair and his pubic hair trailed down from his navel into his shorts.

I took off my shirt and drank some water, I offered him some. He drank and brushed his arm across my leg very slowly when he passed me back the bottle. Then he adjusted his dick. It was a massive curve in his bike shorts. I adjusted mine.

Nothing happened for a minute until he smiled. Then, I touched him and from there it was a massive pile of my body and his rolling around on the ground. We were jacking off, sucking one another's balls, then cumming all over the place.

We finally rode out of the canyon. A perfect, exhausting, exhilarating day.

-C.P. of Los Angeles

THE HOT BUS STOP

Dear **NM**,

In response to your request for nude encounters, I submit the following true story.

It was a very hot sweltering Chicago summer afternoon. I was on my way to work and was standing at the bus stop for a Sheridan bus to take me to the Loop. On the corner about ten feet behind me was a five story apartment building of 1950's vintage. It was the kind of residential building in which the first level is partially sunken below street level. For privacy, the first floor level apartment dwellers generally have their shades drawn to ward off the prying eyes of curious passer-bys.

Anyway, I must have just missed the bus, because I was the only one at the bus stop and nothing was in sight. The heat had driven all but the heartiest off the street. They bus seemed to be taking it's good ole time to arriving, but it didn't matter because I had plenty of time to get to work.

I was standing there, idly musing to myself, when out of the building sauntered a rather handsome white guy.

Mr. Handsome could well have been a GQ model. He was attired for the sweltering weather in simply a pair of sandals, a red midriff tank-top, and a pair of seductively cut-off, hip-hugging Levi Jeans. While he was not overly muscular, his physique left no doubt that he was a gym habitué.

The noise of a loose window shade spinning and flapping around on it's roller and a window tossed open diverted my attention. The sound seemed to come from one of the ground level apartments directly behind me.

I turned in time to see the biggest, tallest, most muscular black man, I have ever laid my eyes on. He must have been over six feet tall and weighed about 230-250 pounds. Clearly, I was looking at the world class beef. As I looked down into the apartment, I could see his body from his knees up.

He appeared to be standing in a bedroom window, because I could discern an unmade bed, chest of drawers, a small vanity table and other similar items of furniture. The only bit of clothing he wore was a blue shower cap on his head. He stood there, naked as a jaybird, with beads of water dripping from his body as if he had just stepped out of a shower.

He had a prodigious piece of uncut sausage swaying from a tangled crop of wiry black hairs. His body just rippled with muscles. Oblivious to me standing there with my mouth agape and eyes agog, he called out to Mr. Handsome, stopping him in his tracks. "Scott, don't forget to buy the dick rubbers!," he yelled.

The unexpected display of black beef elicited a spontaneous applause and shouts of bravo from me. The sudden racket that I generated caused the muscleman to realize that he and his magnificent uncut manhood was totally exposed to public view.

He gave me a broad, embarrassed grin, and with great aplomb he made a low theatrical bow. He then gave me an abrupt thumbs-up signal with his hands. However, I got one last breathtaking view of his rippling ebony muscles, as he quickly re-closed the window and stretched upward to catch the still-flapping window shade to pull it back down.

I turned to see Scott still standing there with an unabashed expression on his face. He sheepishly shrugged his shoulders and answered the unasked question by simply saying, "We can't keep enough of those damned things around the house because Tyrone just fucks me silly." Scott, then turned and continued his journey, while I resumed my wait for the bus...a bit red faced, but dreamily envious.

- A. from Chicago

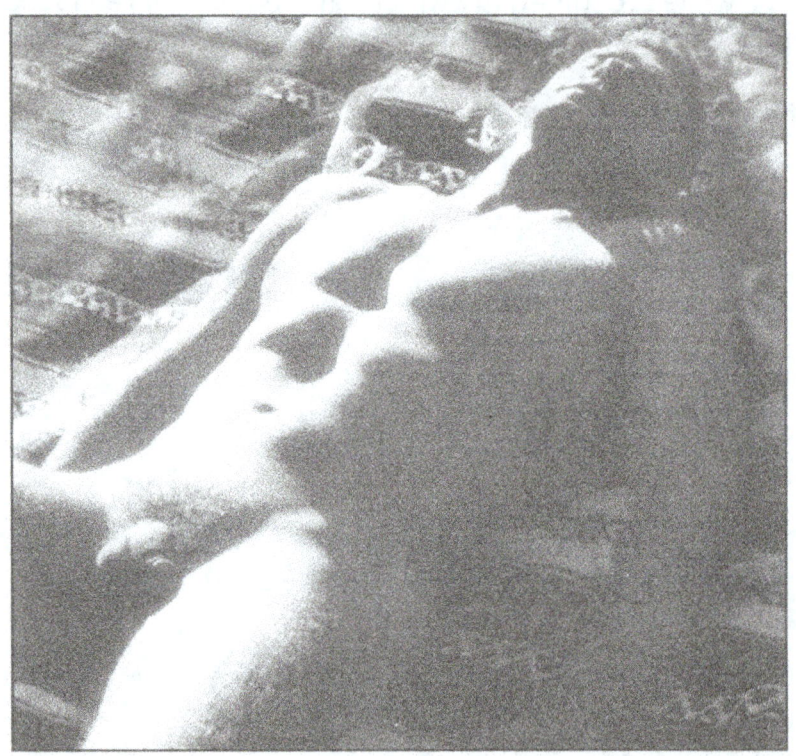

EROTIC JEFF

DEAR **NM**,

Here's a true story that I found to be very erotic at the time it was happening, and fondly remember it now.

I have been friends with this actor for some time. I shall call him Jeff, for this story. He is not generally well-known but has been in several movies and commercials.

I enjoy nudity and so does Jeff. One day he asked me if I wanted to go for a drive up the mountain with him and another one of his friends. I went along and on the way up he stopped and asked his friend to drive.

We were in a large dark-colored van with no windows in the back. While his friend drove, Jeff climbed to the back where a mattress was laid out. He stayed there for a moment and then quietly began to take off his clothes.

Both his friend and I knew he had taken them off. Jeff finally said he felt more comfortable back there naked. I was turned on by it, and I presume, his friend was, too.

Every now and then I would look back at Jeff. He changed position a lot. Sometimes there would be a nice view of his white butt facing me, then a view of his dick. He actually fell asleep on the drive up, which made it even more erotic for me. I liked the fact that he was so comfortable with nudity.

Eventually we stopped and he dressed again. We explored the

mountains all day and finally drove back down to the city. He didn't get naked this time. I guess because he was driving.

Back at Jeff's, we did get into some nice three-way action. It turned out to be a really nice erotic day...thanks Jeff.

-C.A. of Los Angeles, CA

STRIP!

Dear **NM**,

We didn't know we had something in common until one summer day a few years ago. I worked part time at one of the lease shops at a major department store and started up a conversation with a handsome guy in the Halloween shop. Our backgrounds were different but we managed to see a few movies over the winter. Jake was shorter than I and had a great smile - one of those that would make any situation all right.

It had been a few months since I had heard his voice when the phone rang one 90-degree July day. Thinking that his suggestion to go out to the lake and look at the scenery was a good idea, I stopped by his house to pick him up. He was wearing a t-shirt with nylon shorts, the kind you could almost see through, but he was wearing something underneath.

After stopping for a soda and finding a suitable location we passed the Frisbee around. At the first sign of sweat I peeled off my shirt. Jake stopped and watched, then walked over to an adjacent table and did the same. Nice tan, very dark.

After a few more rounds, he came up to me and asked if I minded if he took off his shorts. No, I said and confessed that I had been wishing he would. He dropped them and walked back and placed them with his shirt. I was shocked, and in heaven! What he had on wasn't much and still didn't expose a tan line.

After running after a few more spins I had to give up. The lining on my shorts were loose and I couldn't arrange myself to keep from falling out.

The wind was almost nonexistent and we couldn't stand sitting still. I put my shorts on again and suggested we drive for a while. Jake talked about how he had been waiting for the opportunity and courage to wear less out in public. He seemed excited that he wore his skimpy bathing suit even though I could not see much of an erection through his shorts. It was still affecting me, however. I just ignored the fact that each time I pressed down on the clutch my cock inched out further through the gap in my shorts.

The wind felt nice but it was not enough. For some reason I was feeling extremely hot! At the next stop signal I ripped off my shirt again and said, "Jake, it's so hot, I think you shouldn't be wearing anything at all. " I raised my eyebrows as we pulled away from the intersection. He looked at me with a slight panic in his voice, "what?" I looked back and told him to strip!

A nervous smile spread across his face as he began the experience of his first naked ride. He pulled off his shorts and leaned his seat back. The rays coming through the trees fell through the open sunroof and spotlighted his now raging hard on.

Just having a naked man riding in the car was a new experience for me…I tended to speed up when trucks passed to be ornery. I was certain they could look down though the sunroof and see the same thing I was enjoying. And no, he didn't have a tan-line! (Jake if you are reading, write in and tell your side of it!)

Now I am in the habit of telling him to strip. Sometimes in some unusual places - like on campus of the local university or at the top of a stairwell. I like to find people who are like-minded that he hasn't met yet so we can drop in on. I then whisper in his ear to strip at a seemingly embarrassing moment. Anyone interested?

-Serin from Illinois

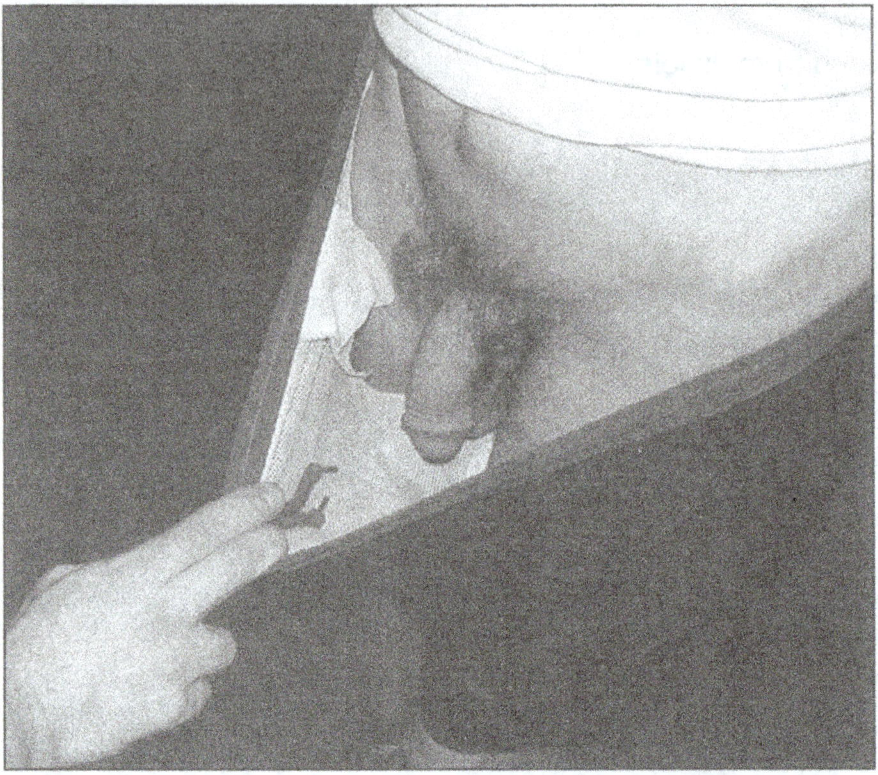

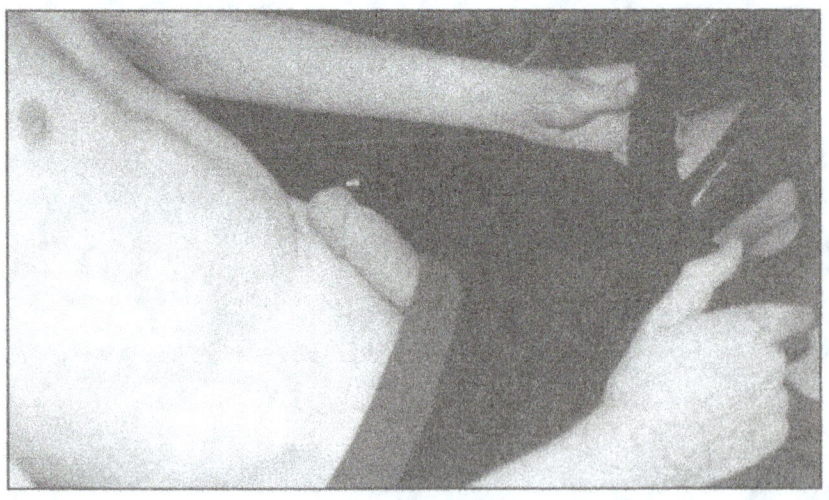

CAR SEX

Dear **NM**,

Visiting an out-of-town city can be frustrating trying to find the "cruisy" areas. It's either a certain section of the city where "the bars" are located or a cruise park or beach.

Visiting Dallas, Texas, in the early eighties for several summers in a row. I stumbled upon Turtle Creek Park, then known for the hottest outdoor sex and exhibition rituals. Early mornings were always open for me and I usually hit the nearest drive-thru, bought breakfast and went to park in a lot behind a baseball diamond. The weather was usually very hot and humid. I sometimes sat in my car with the door open and I would do some paperwork or read for research.

There were times when other guys would be sitting in their cars, listening to their tape players. I didn't think much of it until one day I noticed that two cars were parked with one facing into the slot and the other backed into the slot with the driver's doors open to each other.

I began to be curious and watch a ritual that I have never experienced before -"car sex". Both drivers either were nude or at least stroking off so that the person in the other car could watch. What a turn-on! The two guys were very good-looking and seemed to enjoy having me watch them play. The parking lot was situated such that one could see a car drive in at the other side of the baseball diamond and then see if it was turning onto the long driveway to the parking lot. It allowed enough time to pull up and on any clothes and shut your door and never get caught.

So began my "car sex" voyeurism. One morning during my usual cruise, this one guy in a small pick-up truck came through and parked a space over from me. I played cool because I had heard of undercover police doing things like that. I kept my cool and just sat there listening to my tape player with my earphones.

Every once in a while I'd glance over to see if he was watching me. He was wearing a red baseball cap and silver reflector glasses, no shirt and muscled shoulders and arms. He kept staring straight ahead and didn't seem interested.

Later, he moved his truck to the other side of my car and a space away and parked facing into the space. I then knew he wanted to "play". I saw him look down and he seemed to be fiddling with something. In time, I came to understand that the guy was taking off his shorts and was sitting there naked.

This cat and mouse cruise went on for about forty-five minutes...finally, I decided to relocate. In the time it took to take off my earphones and start up my car, he opened his door. There he was...completely naked and stroking a huge erection and enjoying showing it to me.

I just smiled, turned off the engine and watched the show. Not only did he open the door, he positioned himself so that he could easily step out of his truck and have the door block anyone from seeing him naked. He eventually did stand up, stroke it off to a huge climax and then get back into truck and drive off. I was flabbergasted! I had never experienced anything like that before!

This scene continued on and off all summer with variations...backing in, stripping, getting off and leaving. Always without speaking or saying anything. I had begun to enjoy my early morning car-sex sessions. One morning, I was real horny and sitting there I noticed a truck enter the park, drive around the baseball diamond and into the parking lot. This time there were two guys in the truck. "oh-oh the Police," I thought, "they are going to arrest me."- How wrong I was!

The truck pulled up next to my car. The driver struck up a conversation with me and said the other guy was his roommate. They wanted to show off for me but they wanted me to follow them to another parking spot somewhere in the area.

I was somewhat hesitant to move but I knew they were serious. We left and I followed them to an area behind a modern office building and a warehouse parking area. If you didn't know there was a parking lot behind these two buildings, you would drive right past them and never see the entrance. The parking lot was surrounded by the walls of the warehouse at one end, a railroad track with heavy bushes and trees along the length of a the lot and one end open to a grass field with a high chain-link fence looking out onto an expressway.

It was a Sunday morning so there weren't many people driving around. We backed our cars into the spaces with his "room-mate" on my left and the driver on his other side.

After we got situated, I began to get nervous by the thought that I could be mugged. I was super horny so I pulled off my jogging shorts and t-shirt. No sooner than I stripped, the roommate opened his door and I saw both of them naked there except for baseball caps, tennis shoes and socks.

Their cocks were rock hard and standing up straight. I opened up my door and we flashed for each other. The driver then opened his door, got out and walked around behind his truck to stand between the two cars. The roommate got out and stood there by the truck. They wanted me to get out as well. Not to miss out, I got out of my car and there we were bare-assed naked outside giving each other a show. What a fantastic feeling to be completely naked, outside, showing off with two other hot guys. Eventually, we all came together.

Afterwards, we just laughed and sat there on the side of our cars; making small talk. I eventually had to leave and get on with my day. What I remember of my introduction to "car sex" is that being naked outside was the best feeling of all.

-Allen from NYC

www.ingramcontent.com/pod-product-compliance
Lightning Source LLC
Chambersburg PA
CBHW070042260626
47159CB00005B/2100